Dear Chaotic

(Loving A Chaotic Savage 2)

By: Author Barbie Amor
Formally known as Barbie Scott

This is a work of fiction. All of the characters, organizations, and events portrayed in this novel are either products of the author's imagination or are used fictitiously. Any resemblance to actual persons, living or dead is purely coincidental.

Prologue

"I love you, Amor."

"I love you too." I smiled, loving how he always told me he loved me.

"How much?" he asked, making me laugh.

"Too muthafucking much," I replied, and he chuckled. "TMM, nigga," I added, and this was gonna be my new thing.

"I need a gangsta
To love me better
Than all the others do
To always forgive me
Ride or die with me
That's just what gangsters do..."

"You hungry?" He turned the music down briefly.

"Kinda."

"A'ight, we gon' grab something to eat before we go in." He exited the highway and turned right on Central Avenue. "I'mma slide by my G Mom's house real quick. Put these straps up."

"Okay," I replied, and he started the song over and turned it up.

I loved this song because it reminded me of our love story. It was Kehlani's "Gangsta" from the <u>Suicide Squad.</u> I knew it sounded weird, but Chaotic and I's love story reminded me of The Joker and Harley

Quinn's love story. This man would terrorize the world, and the only thing he loved was Harley Quinn. He was afraid to love, and after Harley basically tortured him with her heart, he had no choice but to love her. Harley loved him to the point he made her jump into acid, and she did. Not being able to hide the love he had grown for her, he jumped in to save her.

"Damn," he said, looking in the rearview mirror, bringing me from my thoughts.

"What?" I asked and looked behind us. There was a patrol car behind us, and it had just turned on its sirens.

"Give me the guns," I told him, and he hesitated. "Canyon, now," I demanded, and he slid them over to me without much movement. I put them into my purse and made sure to take my wallet out in case they wanted my license.

"License and registration," the officer asked, walking up to the car.

Chaotic handed it to the officer, and he stepped away from the car briefly. When he came back, he instructed Chaotic to step out of the car. He looked at me and began shaking his head. He did as told and stepped out of the car. By the time the officer walked him over to the curb, a swarm of officers rushed us and jumped out with their guns drawn.

"Passenger, step out of the car with your hands up!" They began shouting into the bullhorn.

I stepped out of the car with my hands in the air and stepped over to the curb. After a few moments, the officers rushed Chaotic and didn't dare cuff me. A female officer wrapped her arm into mine and pulled me to the side.

"Canyon Betterman, you're under arrest for the murder of Karter Barkley." I heard an officer say, and it made me spin around fast.

Karter Barkley. I repeated the words as if I hadn't heard him correctly. I looked at Chaotic, and our eyes met. There was so much regret in his eyes that it made me dizzy. We continued to hold each other's gaze, and a pool of tears began to fall from my eyes. I had to be dreaming. No, fuck that. I had to be having a nightmare. My heart began fluttering with pain, and I couldn't help but look Chaotic in the eyes. When the officers snatched him up and walked him to the car, I followed him with my eyes every step of the way.

They stuffed him down into the car, and another officer climbed into the driver seat and wasted no time pulling off. All of the other officers got into their vehicles leaving me standing here. I didn't know what to do next because I was still in shock. They never searched me, and this told me they got exactly what they wanted.

When I finally came to, I climbed into my car and sat here for what felt like forever. The sound of my phone snapped me out of it, and because it was Ru, I let it go to voicemail. I started my engine, and before I could pull off, I began screaming at the top of my lungs…

"Noooooooooooooooo!"

❤️□□□

For three days, I buried myself inside my bedroom in tears. It was hard because Ru couldn't figure out what was wrong, and I knew I was killing him. Everything that happened was hard to process, and my heart still ached. A part of me wanted answers, but the other part of me wanted blood. I wanted to kill Chaotic for more than one reason. I asked myself if he knew this entire time and was this all a set up to begin with. I didn't understand why. I mean, I knew I was his enemy, but I ain't deserve no shit like that. I gave that man my heart, and not only that, but my love. The way he told me he loved me was what had me caught up. He looked so sincere. It couldn't be fake. I began to cry again and buried my head into my pillow.

When my phone began ringing, I didn't have the strength to answer. I knew it could only be Misha or Jami because I had told them what happened.

(713) 297-6111

I looked at the number that wasn't stored and answered.

"Hello?"

"This is global tel. You have a prepaid call from 'Chaotic.' To accept, press five. To deny charges, hang up now, or to block all future calls, dial zero."

Hearing his voice made my blood begin to boil. It took everything in me not to push five and curse him out. However, I couldn't face him. I knew my little brother wasn't the intended victim, but it happened, and I'd never get him back. For years, it fucked with me, and I always promised myself if I found out who pulled the trigger, they were dead.

Fuck Chaotic.

I got up from my bed and headed into the restroom. When I looked into the mirror, my eyes were puffy from crying, and I looked like a lost soul. I began washing my face and tried hard to get myself together. It was time I faced Ru, but I wasn't gonna tell him the truth.

I took slow steps toward the living room, and with every step, my heart rate sped up. When I turned the corner, my hands began to shake, but a sense of calm came over me when I looked at my daughter. Ru sat on the sofa with Heaven in his arms. I sat back for a moment and just watched them. It was evident in Ru's face that I had broken him down to the point of no return. I knew I'd stressed him out over a course of months, but no matter what, he deserved it. I guess after all this, it made me open my eyes to reality. Chaotic was really the myth I always pictured him to be. I guess the Harley and Joker story did remind me of us because it was all a tale. My life was right here with Ru, and it was time we had that talk.

I took a seat next to Ru, and neither of us said a word. I turned to face him as I searched for the right words. I let out a soft sigh and turned my whole body around so he could look at me.

"So what you wanna do? You wanna fix this, or just let it go?" I asked seriously. If he chose to let go, then I was fine with that because maybe I needed to be alone.

"Let's fix it," he spoke, and for the first time, I heard sincerity in his voice.

"You wanna move?"

"Yep. Let's go."

"Okay," I replied, and that was all I needed to hear.

I lifted up from the sofa and headed into my bedroom. I sat on the bed and began contemplating my next move. It was time I took my family away from here, and maybe it would help Ru and I's relationship. There was nothing in the city for us, and the way my heart felt, I needed to escape the pain. I needed to find a way to protect my peace, and staying here wasn't gonna work. Therefore, I was gonna start looking for a home a couple hours away. I guess this was what it was gonna be. Who would have ever thought that my fate would end with Ruger?

Chapter 1 Chaotic

UNITED STATES OF AMERICA,
Plaintiff.

VS.

CANYON M BETTERMAN,
Defendant.

"Your Honor, this is the sixth month we've been waiting for discovery. The witness has not been located, and all we have is an informant statement."

"Mr. Ogilby, where's your witness?"

"He's, ummm...ummm...we haven't found him, Your Honor. We just need about another week or so."

"My defendant has been wrongly accused, we have no witness, no firearm, and he's been detained for six months. Your Honor, I'd like to file a motion for a dismissal."

"I want to contest. I'll have the discovery by the end of the week."

"Well, we're gonna set the next court date for October ninth."

The Judge banged his gavel, and everyone stood to their feet. A CO quickly called me over to cuff me and escorted me to the holding tank. I shook my head the entire way there because a nigga had to sit in this bitch another month. It'd been six months since I was arrested, and without one piece of evidence, I was a sitting duck. The only thing they had was a witness who they couldn't locate. A part of me wanted to fire my attorney because the money-hungry bitch wasn't fighting for me in my eyes. However, because I've paid her off, I decided to keep her around.

Walking back into the cell, my mind was racing with anticipation. I had niggas in the streets on an assignment because the witness who was responsible was dead. On the transcript they had, the name was covered in bold, so I didn't know who it could be. Whoever it was, I wasn't playing with the nigga, and if I made it out before the police got ahold of him, I was gon' make the bitch pay; off with his head.

"Betterman, you wanna make a call?"

I looked up at a CO by the name of Ms. James. I nodded my head *yes* because I ain't have too much of shit to say to these people. I didn't give a fuck how nice some portrayed to be; they all were enemies in the same clothing.

When I picked up the phone, my first intention was to call Cedes, but for some reason, I dialed Amor. I waited for the operator to finish, then stated my name. When the phone paused for a short moment, I could hear Amor's voice grace the phone, and my heart dropped. Just as I figured, she hung up. I let out a sigh because I guessed my hopes were up high. I mean, I understood why she was upset, but she needed to understand I wasn't responsible. I really ain't know how I was gonna convince her it wasn't me. Because then, I would have to give up who did it, and one thing I wasn't was a rat. I lived by the code of the streets, and whether it was her or the police, I just couldn't do it.

The day they took me replayed in my mind from the moment I picked her up. All I could think about was making love to her on the beach, and each time I thought of that moment, it pained me. After serving her with this dick, and the way she told me she loved me, my intentions were to take her from her nigga and move her out the hood.

I shook my head just thinking about how the police fucked up my plans. When they mentioned the name Karter Barkely, the info didn't register until I looked at Amor. The hurt in her eyes, and the tears that fell rapidly down her face, confirmed it was her little brother. I couldn't do shit but shake my head as vivid thoughts of that night her brother was killed consumed my mind.

We were in the park when the ghetto bird began hovering in the air. Because Amor's and I's hoods were only a few blocks away, I could see the bird and hear the sirens clearly. I knew the homies had went down there. Because earlier that day, some of them niggas came through and shot the park up. When they made it back, I knew something wasn't right because they looked too stressed out. They approached the crowd, and one of the homies spoke in a low tone.

"We hit a kid."

I looked at him to see if I heard him right, and before I could ask, another homie asked first.

"Nigga, y'all hit a kid?" he asked, and he nodded yes.

"Is he dead?" I asked, praying he said no.

Now when it came to this gang-banging shit, I'd kill a woman, but kids were unacceptable. *The reason I'd kill a bitch was because these bitches these days were tougher than some of these niggas. Bitches like Amor and that dike bitch she was always with were prime examples.*

"I saw the little nigga go down," *the homie spoke, and the look in his eyes told me the kid was, in fact, dead. He just ain't want to admit it.* "Man, I ain't even see the little nigga. It's like he came out of no-where," *he added, and dropped his head.*

"And it looked like a car was following us," *the homie who was with him added and dropped his head also.*

"Damn," *was all I could say because the hood was about to be hot, and the war was gonna get heated. Not to mention, if someone did follow them, they could have gotten the plate number.* "I hope you nig-gas ready to go to war."

I looked each of them in the eyes and began to read 'em. Already, I could see the fear in their eyes, and it wasn't just from the full-blown war that was about to take place. It was also from the police who weren't gonna stop until they had someone in custody.

"Hello?" Cedes' voice came through the phone, bringing from a daze.

"Aye, you handle that business?"

"Yeah."

"A'ight. You put that money on my books?"

"Umm-huh."

"A'ight," I responded. Because just that fast, she knocked my energy off. It was bad enough I was in this situation, and still, this bitch never made shit any better.

I disconnected the phone and placed a call to Amor one last time. I knew she wasn't gonna answer, but at least I could hear her voice. A nigga was missing the fuck out of her, and hearing the news about her and her nigga moving crushed me. I knew there was a possibility that it was too late, and they had worked out their problems. But her answering every so many calls gave me a little hope. That same feeling I always had didn't change. I didn't give a fuck if the nigga married her and put another baby in her. I was coming for my bitch.

Chapter 2 Amor

"**H**appy birthday to you...happy birthday to you... happy birthday, Heaven... happy birthday to you!"

Everyone began clapping and cheering as Heaven's dad tried to help her blow out her candle. It was her first birthday, and we decided to do something in our new home with a small crowd. Ru's mother had come to help out, along with his grandmother and a few of his cousins. Misha and Rawdy had pulled up on me, and Jami, with her bad ass kids, were on the way.

Today was the first time everyone had visited Ru and I's new home. We had moved out two hours from the city in the middle of nowhere. As for me, I loved it. I found the peace I had been craving, and the serenity that surrounded me gave me a sense of calm.

Now Ru, on the other hand, I noticed a slight change in his attitude. At first, he was excited about the move, but because he couldn't be near the hood, he had begun to get moody again. For the most part, I made sure we had fun at home, but I guessed it wasn't good enough.

The house had four bedrooms, three bathrooms, and a loft. The backyard was huge and equipped with a pool. Inside the loft, I turned it into a movie theater, and in one of the bedrooms, Ru made it a game room with a pool table and a couple arcade machines. The kitchen was perfect, and because I loved to cook, I purchased a stove with a griddle.
We spent most of our time in the backyard, so almost every weekend, we'd barbeque.

A few homies would always drive up to visit, and it seemed like that was the only time Ru was happy. The way he began to act almost made me regret moving so far, but fuck that. I loved my house, and I needed this. Wasn't shit in the city for me, and it was a better place to raise my daughter.

Although Ru and I tried hard to work on ourselves, it was like my feelings just weren't the same. I tried hard to fall back in love with him, but because of the loss of attraction, everything remained the same; he just wasn't into me. No matter how many candles I lit, the lingerie I wore, or how good I tried to suck his dick, the nigga just wasn't catering to my heart as he should. I mean, he acted happy when we were out spending my money. However, moment we'd walk back into our home, it was like he'd leave the good energy at the door.

I couldn't even front and say the shit didn't bother me because it did, however, I found serenity within myself. I knew how to make myself happy. Most days I spent my time around the house working on my online boutique, cooking, and listening to my Anita Baker. I would tune Ru out and vibed around the house with a glass of Hennessy.

"Amor, yo' phone." Misha pointed to my ringing phone that

set on the table. The look she was giving me was one of those *bitch, get yo' phone before yo' nigga see it* looks, and that told me exactly who the call was from.

I quickly picked up my phone and looked over to Ru. When I noticed he wasn't looking, I walked away and headed into the kitchen.

When I answered, I waited for the operator to finish speaking, and Chaotic's voice came blaring through the phone. Just like any other time, I wanted so badly to push five and accept, but I just couldn't do it. I wanted to curse his ass out, but because of the embarrassment, I didn't have shit to say to him. I hung up the phone and let out a deep sigh. Just hearing his voice always did something to me I couldn't describe. It was one of those bittersweet moments, and this was why I answered.

"I'm telling you, ma, that nigga wasn't one of the shooters."

I turned around startled by Rawdy's voice. I sighed again seeing that it was her, and I took in what she was saying. I watched her momentarily, and something in her eyes told me she was sure.

"He wouldn't be in jail. They had to have some type of evidence against him, Rawdy."

"True, but I know Chaotic, and I'm telling you, it wasn't that nigga," she defended with that same sure look.

This was the third time Rawdy tried to vouch for Canyon, but I didn't care. There had to be some sort of evidence that not only made them arrest him but to keep him. It'd been six months since then. There would have been a dismissal by now, yet there wasn't. The only thing that made me wanna believe Rawdy was how she hated Chaotic and his hood. Therefore, she could just say fuck him and let me, just as the justice system, believe it was him, but she didn't.

"Well, that's for the justice system to determine. And if the nigga makes it out, I'mma kill him myself."

"Girl, you in love with that nigga. You ain't gon' kill shit." She shook her head, but I was serious.

I turned around to dismiss her, and Ru was standing there

with an awkward look on his face. Rawdy and I looked at each other, then to Ru. I wasn't sure how much he'd heard, but he was looking dead at me.

"We about to open the gifts, shorty," Ru said, and I nodded *okay.*

I let out the breath of air I was holding the moment he walked back out. Rawdy and I looked at each other again, and we held each other's gaze. I knew she wanted to say something else, but because of Ru, she kept it to herself. She walked out of the kitchen, and I stood behind to process it all.

My phone rang again, and this time, it startled me. I looked at the caller ID, and it was Chaotic. Too afraid Ru would walk in, I let it go to voicemail. I clutched the phone tightly and closed my eyes while sighing. For some reason, it was like the air that escaped my lungs came from my heart. I was in a fucked up situation. Not a day went by that I didn't think of the moments. Fuck him, per se. It was the moments that put me in some sort of trance. I couldn't escape the thoughts of our sexscapade, or even the thoughts of him invading my space.

Then I'd think about Karter, and I'd get mad. My little brother's death was something I couldn't stomach for years. And to know the man I was in love with was held responsible was sickening.

I shook the thoughts away and walked out the kitchen for my baby. When I saw her big, pretty eyes light up, it made me smile and redirected my energy to what was going on today. It was my baby's first birthday, and a day to remember.

Chapter 3 Amor

I didn't know why, but a bitch was horny as hell and ready for some dick. After taking a candle lit bath, while having a glass of wine, I was really in the mood. I slid into some lingerie and lit the rest of the candles around my room. I turned on my Monica Pandora station and grabbed my glass. I prepared myself for the energy in the next room. I walked out of my room and went up to the loft to chill with Ru. He was playing his game, so I was hoping, in this outfit, I'd snatch his attention.

I headed up the stairs, and at first, he didn't look my way. I watched as he went up for a jumper, and when he made it, he looked behind him.

"Damn," he said. He looked at the TV, then looked back again. "Oh, you tryna get hit…" He paused his game and smirked.

"You playing yo' game." I smirked back.

I sat in one of the theater chairs and crossed my legs sexily. I took a sip from my glass and watched Ru play his game. He had two minutes left, and because he was up by fifteen points, I knew he would win and wouldn't be mad. He was currently playing in a *2k* tournament, so this game was serious. He ain't pay my ass any more attention, so once the game was over, I made my way downstairs.

I climbed into bed and opened my laptop. I began fooling around with my website that I was currently working on until I dozed off.

When I opened my eyes, the sun was peeking in, and Ru was standing over me closing my laptop. After he set it down, he climbed into bed and began rubbing my ass. I scooted over in the opposite direction to let him know I ain't wanna be bothered. He waited for me to doze off, and he tried to make a move. Already knowing Ru, I didn't fall into a deep sleep.

However, when I opened my eyes, he had his dick oiled up going inside of me. Instead of complaining, I lifted my ass and tooted my leg. I let him do him until I was ready for him to bust, so I could go back to sleep. I began throwing my ass in small circles as I squeezed my pussy muscles. Within minutes, he began howling like a damn wolf and bust a fat nut inside of me. I jumped up from the bed and went to pee, so I could get all the nut out of me. Afterward, I washed up and climbed back into the bed. Ru got up to do the same thing, then came back to lie down. When he climbed into the bed, I kicked my leg over him just as I'd always done.

"Un-un…move that big muthafucka," he complained, making me smack my lips.

Wow. Nigga still acting weird even after I gave him my pussy. I just scooted away from him and fluffed my pillow to get some sleep. Keep shit real, I wasn't even mad because this had become a routine in our home. Like I said, the first few months were great. I thought Ru and I were doing great up until he began missing them streets. I asked him on many occasions if he was so unhappy, why was he here? Instead of saying things like, "Babe, I'm happy," or "I wouldn't trade this for the world," the nigga would always say, "What are you talking about? I'm cool."

But, no he wasn't, and it was evident on his face daily. It was like slowly, he was beginning to transform back to the nigga from the old house. It did kinda hurt me at first because I moved us out here for a change—in hopes things would get better for us. Not to mention, I spent at least 15k on the move, and he didn't bother giving me a dime. I re-furnished the entire house and made sure to make it comfortable enough for him. But, nah. None of that was good enough.

Knowing I wasn't going back to sleep, I began scrolling through my phone. Because I was a big Google head, I went to Google and began reading the daily news. After nearly an hour of just surfing the web, I didn't know why, but I went to inmate search.

LASD Inmate Search

Last Name: Betterman First Name: Canyon

The Los Angeles County **Sheriff's Department** Welcome to *Inmate Information Center*

Search For Another Inmate   Back To The Search Result

Booking No.: B65016731 Last Name: **Betterman** First Name: **Canyon** Middle Name: **M**

Sex: **M** Race: **H** Date Of Birth: **01/31/1994** Age: **27** Hair: **BLK** Eyes: **BRO** Height: **510** Weight: **175** Charge Level: **M**

(Felony)

Arrest Date: **02/14/2018** Arrest Time: **7:36AM** Arrest Agency: **421754** Agency Description: **LAPD-DIVISION** Date Booked: **02/15/2018**

Time Booked: **1533** Booking Location: **427953** Location Description: **LAPD - COUNTY JAIL (LA)**

Total Bail Amount: **$1,000,000**

Next Court Code: Next Court Date: **10/09/2018** Next Court Time: **0830**

Court Name: **LA SUPERIOR CT DEPT I**
Court Address: **900 THIRD STREET** Court City: **LOS ANGELES**

I read over the information on Chaotic and took a screen-shot. I also noticed a court date coming next month. A part of me wanted to go, but knowing how them courtrooms worked, I wouldn't be able to stomach any photos of my brother lying there dead. I thanked God my mother was out of state because she would have definitely showed up. She called me a week after Chaotic's arrest and told me they had a possible suspect. I pretended I didn't know because how could I tell my mother I was with the man who possibly murdered her child, and he even got taken into custody out of my car?

I prayed like hell I wouldn't come up in his transcripts. Because not only my mother, but then Ru would know I was with him. However, they never asked me my name. The day it all happened, Ruger did ask about the guns I had, so I made up a lie about holding them for Rawdy. Of course, I called her to give her a heads up, and Rawdy being Rawdy, she never questioned the fact that I was lying. I wasn't sure what I was gonna do with them, but for now, I had them stashed in my new home.

Chapter 4 Chaotic

"**B**etterman, the witness is in custody." My attorney looked at me and shook her head. "If he or she is credible, this could injure the case. Are you familiar with a Tyson Frank?"

I looked at her, not believing my ears. I nodded my head in shock hoping there was another Tyson Frank in the world.

"Well, he's here. The police located him a week ago. More than likely, they're gonna just subpoena him to come back for trial. And you better believe they're gonna put him into some sort of witness protection until this is over."

I didn't know if I was tripping, but she gave me a crazy look as if she either knew I wanted to kill him, or she wanted the nigga dead her damn self.

"That nigga won't be credible," I assured, her knowing his bitch ass couldn't say too much of nothing.

He knew why, and the nigga was lucky I wasn't a rat. I knew exactly why he was doing what he was doing, and I was sure he was tryna get me out the way. He thought he could just wee tip them and he'd be clear, but the way the LAPD worked, yo' ass was coming in as a witness. No matter how many promises they made to keep it confidential, yo' ass was getting on that stand. Dumb nigga there.

I stood up with confidence. I wasn't gonna let that hoe deter me from having faith. I had to get to Amor and wasn't shit gonna stop me; therefore, I was determined to beat this case and prove to her it wasn't me.

"There's one more witness. She says she was there. I was able to speak to her, and she couldn't identify you, which is good. Let's go, Betterman." She grabbed her briefcase and headed out the room.

Seconds later, a CO walked in and escorted me to the courtroom. When we walked in, I took my seat next to my attorney. The moment the judge came out, they began. My attorney sat back with me as the DA went over his motions. I anticipated the moment he called his witnesses because this shit was gonna be comical. He mentioned the female witness wasn't here today, but his main witness was.

I watched as Tuck's bitch ass walked out the backroom escorted by a sheriff. The nigga didn't look my way until he was on the stand. I looked him in his eyes and smirked. He quickly turned his head and looked at the judge. The fear in this nigga's eyes was preposterous.

"Your Honor, we would like to place our witness in a protection program for his safety. Mr. Betterman is a very dangerous man with rank in the streets."

"Granted." The judge began to write on a piece of paper granting the protection without a second thought. He then looked at Tuck. "Tyson Frank, you are ordered to appear in court for trial."

"I ain't tryna come." Tuck was turning his head side to side like he was ready to cry.

"Well, I can keep you in custody if you'd like." The judge removed his glasses and looked at him seriously.

Tuck rolled his neck, and I laughed. His best bet was the witness protection because he wouldn't be protected on the streets or behind these walls.

I looked at the nigga one last time, and I wondered if Cedes knew about this this. I couldn't say much on the phone, so I wasn't gonna mention it. However, I was gonna shoot a kite to one of my homies who was here. I was gon' have the nigga call my moms and deliver the message so she could let my brother know. I swear this nigga betta hope that witness protection program protected his ass because if any of my goons got ahold of him, he was done.

❤️🖤🖤🖤

After talking to Cedes, who ain't have shit to say, I hung her up in minutes and called my wife. The first time she ain't answer, but the second time, I could hear her voice say hello through the phone. I stayed on the line, assuming she'd hang up, but to my surprise, she accepted.

"What?" she answered annoyed, and I froze.

I imagined her pretty ass face, and no matter how rude she was acting, I knew this girl; she loved a nigga.

"Look, ma, I ain't kill yo' brother. You gotta believe me. I don't need a rebuttal out of you, so just listen. I really love you. Ain't shit that happened between us fake or some type of game, so get that shit out yo' head. I apologize for being put in this situation and hurting you, but, ma, I ain't do it. On my daddy grave, I ain't do it, and on my daddy grave, when I beat my case, I'm coming to marry you." I hung up without giving her a chance to speak.

I walked back to my cell with not only confidence but emotionally uplifted.

When I got back to my cell, my bunky was on his bed reading a letter.

"You talked to her?' he asked without looking up.

I stepped fully into my cell and jumped on the top bunk. I let out a sigh that confirmed exactly what he asked.

"So what she say?"

"I really ain't give her a chance to say shit. I was just trying to get her to understand it wasn't me. Other than that, I told her I was coming to snatch her ass up when I beat this shit."

I lay my head back on the wall and listened as OG begin talking. Every night, the conversation was always about love. He had a wife he'd been with for nearly twenty years, and because of his love for the streets, he was on a path of losing her. No matter how much shit OG got himself into, that girl was always there to hold him down. He always told me about every bid he had done, and no matter the countless women, the countless court dates, or the countless years he'd already spent behind bars, Alonya was always by his side. He also told me stories about his addiction to drugs and the passion he had grown for the white girl. He told me how he made love to the glass pipe and neglected his wife while doing it. This go around, he was facing a murder charge on another crackhead he had killed over a bike Downtown. I could tell for the first time, it finally hit him, and he knew Alonya was fed up with his shit.

"One thing I always had, youngsta, was an addiction to those streets. I took what I had at home for granted, and now that I'm on the losing end, for the first time in life, I regret everything I've ever done. Alonya didn't deserve nothing I put her through, man. But I couldn't help it. Them streets kept calling me. It don't be the craving for drugs, it's the thrill of the streets. When you make it out of this situation, do what you gotta do to make you a better man. Not a hood nigga, Canyon, because the hood ain't gon' love you back, but a better man for that girl. From what you tell me, y'all both been through some shit, so it's time y'all found love and peace in your lives. I'm sure that's why she ran off with that other brother." He pointed and scrunched his lips. "To find peace. But I bet you ain't a day that goes by you don't cross her mind. That's the one for you."

"And how you know that?"

"Because the heart wants what the heart wants. I wanted the streets, and look where I'm at. You want Love, and that's what you gon' get."

I chuckled because no matter what, he always called Amor *Love* instead of her name.

"If God gives you a second chance, choose love." He closed his eyes, and I knew he was thinking of his wife.

Instead of replying, I closed my eyes and fell into a daze. It was crazy how I thought of Amor more than my case. Many nights, I lay on this bunk, and I'd ask God to bring me home to her. I was looking at a life sentence behind some shit I ain't do, but this could possibly be my karma. They had Tuck as a witness and wasn't no telling what that female witness saw or what she'd say.

The day I was arrested, they raided my crib and found a gun. Instead of Cedes saying it was hers, she told them it was mine, so they booked it in as evidence. After performing an analysis on it, it was clean, so they didn't have a murder weapon; that was the only thing helping me. I knew if I didn't beat this case, Amor would think it was me, and she'd definitely hate me. If that day came, it was out of my control, and *the streets* won; just like OG said.

Chapter 5 Amor

Six Months Later

I opened my eyes to the smell of bacon that had tickled my nose. We got fucked up last night and fell asleep head to head on the sofa, so because she wasn't right here, I knew it was her in the kitchen. I got up and went to handle my hygiene, then headed into the kitchen. Jami was moving around with Betty Wright blasting in the air. The house was bright from the blinds being pulled back, and to my surprise, it was nice and quiet. Normally when I woke up in Jami's home, the sound of her children running through the halls could be heard.

"Morning, friend." She turned around, then grabbed two glasses. "Set these on the table, so I can make our plates." She handed me the glasses, then began making our plates.

We both took a seat at the table and began making small talk. I kept finding myself drifting into a zone every time my attention went outside. It was 8:11 in the morning, and the grey clouds confirmed it was gonna rain soon. The shit was only adding to my gloomy thoughts of Chaotic. I picked up the glass that contained a mimosa and drank a gulp. I began picking through my food as Jami tore into her plate as if she hadn't eaten in days.

"I'm starving. That damn drank last night."

I couldn't help but laugh because we drank all night, and this girl woke us up with mimosas. Before I could reply, my phone began ringing, and my heart dropped. I knew it was Canyon because he called every morning at the same time. Some days I'd answer just to hear him say his name, then I'd hang up.

The moment I said hello into the phone, Jami looked at me as if she knew it was him.

"Answer it, friend," she spoke sympathetically, then dropped her head to continue eating.

"Hello?" I answered and waited for the operator to finish before I pressed five.

"I love you, ma," Chaotic spoke into the phone, and I could hear in his voice he was drained out.

I didn't reply.

"I'm 'bout to start trial soon. If God allows it and I beat this case, I'm coming to get you." He disconnected the line just as he had done the last time I accepted the call.

It reminded me of when he was out. He would dip in, talk shit, and dip right out. It was like loving me frustrated him, but he couldn't resist.

"Damn, what he say?" Jami asked, looking at me curiously.

"Nothing, really. If he beats his case, he's coming for me."

We both got silent and took a sip from our glasses.

"What's up with Ru?" She changed the subject.

"Same shit. Home being dad, while I run the streets."

I shrugged because it was true. Over the last few months, I had begun coming to the city to escape Ru. I'd stay at hotels or right here at Jami's. I'd be gone for days at a time, and not once would he call to see if I was okay. Things at home with Ru were just as they were in our old home. Keep shit real, it seemed like things were worse.

"His ass just ain't gon' learn." She shook her head. "So I guess y'all ain't having a wedding?"

"Hell no. I been changed my mind about that. It's only one man on earth I'd marry, and that's a myth. Therefore, I ain't ever getting married."

"And who's that?" She smirked, already knowing the answer.

"Chaotic," I replied sternly.

Again, we both got silent, and this gave me time to contemplate my answer. I couldn't front; Chaotic was the only man on this Earth I craved. Like I said, being with him was a myth, so I knew it would never happen. I knew I loved the nigga because no man had ever made my body feel as he did. And for some reason, a part of me had that faith that he didn't murder my brother.

"What if it's true?" Jami asked just above a whisper.

I knew she was referring to Chaotic killing Karter, and that question was on point with my thoughts.

"Then I guess the fairytale ends."

I looked out the window just as the drizzles began sliding down the glass window. I couldn't even hold back if I wanted to; a lone tear slid down my face, and my heart began crying a river. I looked at Jami, and this was why I loved her. She was always in tune with my emotions. A small tear fell from her eye, and she gave me time to regroup.

"I miss him," I told her dolefully, and it was true. However, things were complicated.

❤□□□

"What's up with this?"

"With what, Ru?" I rolled my eyes and looked at him. He was holding my phone, waiting for me to reply. "What about it?"

"Why you got screenshots of this nigga's court dates and shit in yo' phone?"

"What you mean?" I looked at him as if he had lost his fucking mind. I didn't bother taking my phone from him like I normally did because I was at the point that he could go through the whole thing. If he wanted to pretend like he gave a fuck and got his feelings hurt, that was on him. "I wanna know what's going on with my brother's case," I lied in a sense.

I mean, I did wanna keep up with the case, but those screenshots were for my own personal reasons.

"So what's going on with it? That nigga do it?"

"I don't know. He's starting trial next week."

Ru handed me my phone, and I got up from the bed.

"Heaven and I going to the city," Ru said as I made my way to the restroom that was located in our bedroom.

"Okay. I'm going too. Y'all can drop me off."

"A'ight, we'll, get dressed," he replied, and he didn't have to tell me twice.

I headed to my closet and pulled out some army green Air Max, a pair of skin-tight army green jeans, and a white shirt that fit my body showcasing a bit of my breasts. Because it was still raining, I was gonna wear my army green puffy coat with the fur collar attached. I was wearing a curly bun high on my head thanks to the rain that wouldn't let up.

After I was done with my shower, I began brushing my hair up, then slid into my clothing. Heaven was already dressed, and because her hair was braided to the side, I didn't have to tackle her to the ground to comb it.

Ru walked in dressed as if he had a date, and keep shit real, that was his business. These days, I didn't care enough to care. If he was cheating, I would never know because those going through his phone days were over. He was the one who found the need to touch my shit expecting to find something.

After locking the house up, we all headed out to the car and climbed in. Ru put Heaven in her car seat while I began adjusting the music. Because I was in the car with Ru, I didn't play my normal R&B. I turned to Meek Mills' Pandora station, and the first song came on was "1942." I turned it up as Ru climbed into the driver seat and fastened his belt.

Our two hour drive to the city was gonna be like the typical boring ride, so I began scrolling through my Facebook. Because I knew Ru was focused on the road, I snuck on Chaotic's page to see who had been posting on his wall. There were a few *Free Chaotic* posts, a few bullshit tags of music and memes, and his son, who had left a cute *Free My Pops* post. I continued down his entire page until I reached an old video he was tagged in by his girlfriend. I rolled my eyes as I watched the video with no sound because of Ru.

I didn't know why, but I clicked on her name, and it took me to her page. I began scrolling down her page, and a video stopped me in my tracks. I pressed play and watched as Mercedes was in a full-blown make out session with some brown-skinned nigga. The caption read *Me & Bae,* and this blew me back. All along, I thought he and his girl had made up, and she was holding shit down. Now that could have been the case, and she was just on some player shit. I mean, it wasn't like Canyon would know because he was behind bars. The bitch was bold if you asked me because niggas in jail found out shit faster than on the streets. I quickly left her page, and a part of me was irritated. Chaotic wasn't the type of nigga to be made a fool. He was that nigga, and I was sure she knew just as the streets.

Chapter 6 Amor

After climbing out of the car with Ru, I made sure to kiss my daughter. Ru was heading to his grandma's house, so I had him drop me off in the hood. I had already placed a call to my girls so we could turn the fuck up today. It was only a few minutes after noon, and already, there was a yard full of homies.

Boss was standing amongst the crowd, but he didn't bother looking my way. Since the night we had it out about Chaotic, we hadn't said much to each other. I was still shocked he never told Ru, but that didn't change the way I felt. In my eyes, it was fuck him. Therefore, I was gonna ignore the nigga and turn the fuck up.

"Lady Ru!" Rawdy shouted, excited to see me.

Moments later, Misha jumped from the back seat of her own car, and it looked like a chronic video shoot. The clouds of smoke followed her out of the car as she ran in my direction.

"Hey, bitchhh!"

"Hey, ma."

We hugged as if we hadn't seen each other in years. Although I was in the hood a lot, since I had moved, Misha always told me how much she missed me, and vice versa. Now it was just her and Rawdy, but Rawdy was spending more time with her boo.

"We going up tonight, or nah?"

"Hell yeah. You called the homies?"

"Yep. Let's go get some bottles," I told her, and we headed for the store.

By the time we got back, there was a yard full of people, and everyone who pulled up had liquor. Misha and I opened our first bottle, and for the rest of the day, it was fun and laughs. Rawdy brought up Chaotic a few times, but each time, I changed the subject. I really ain't wanna think about him because I had to stay on point. I didn't know why, but I had an eerie feeling I was trying hard to ignore. I didn't know what the feeling was, but I was gonna direct my energy to enjoying my night, and that was just what I did. By the time I looked up, the sun had gone down, and more people had come.

"So where's Ru? He's coming back to get you?"

"Nah. I'mma stay out tonight."

"Okay, well, if you need me to come back and get you, just call." Jami started her engine and began to let her car warm up.

"Okay. Thanks, friend."

I began walking away, and she called out to me.

"Friend!"

I turned around and looked through the passenger side of her car window.

"Be careful."

"I sure will." I smiled and watched as her car pulled off from the curb.

♥☐☐☐

It was now four in the morning, and I was good and drunk. Misha had gone home, and Rawdy was getting her some pussy from her new boo. It was now just me and three homies finishing the last of our bottle before we parted ways. I had already asked Big Nose Mike to drop me off at Jami's because it was too late for her to come outside.

I looked at my phone for the last time, and I couldn't help but think of how Ru hadn't bothered calling. He didn't ask if I had somewhere to lay my head, was I hungry, or did I even have a ride. This shit was normal, but for some reason, I was in my feelings. Like, damn, nigga. Not once did he even pull up to hang out, and there was a yard full of homies he fucked with heavy.

"Watch this car." I heard Mike's voice, which made me look up.

Just as I looked up, I was staring down the barrel of a MP5. My feet froze, and my heart dropped. I watched as the few homies began to scatter. The sound of the first few shots brought me to, so I took off running down what we called the hall. The hall was a tunnel that led from one side of the street to another, and it was used to park cars.

Pop! Pop! Pop! Pop! Pop! Pop! Pop! Pop! Pop! Pop! Pop! Pop! Pop! Pop! Pop! Pop! Pop! Pop! Pop! Pop! Pop! Pop! Pop! Pop!

As I continued to run, I looked back, and I swear the shooter was aiming right for me. The sudden heat to my leg made me slightly buckle. I could feel a gush of liquid begin to pour, but no matter what, I wasn't gonna stop running. I continued to run until I made it through the hall, then hit the brick wall that led me into another building. Once I made it over, I lay on the ground and began dialing Ru's number. I called over and over, and not once did he answer the phone. I was so in and out of it I didn't hear the homie's voice until he was standing near the wall screaming my name.

"I'm right here!" I called out to him, and he jumped over.

"You hit?"

"Yeah, in my leg," I told him, and he swooped me up into his arms.

He ran in full speed to the yard we all hung out in and began knocking on one of the residents' doors.

"Come in," a Hispanic man named Alejandro told us.

We went inside, and Alejandro ran off to the back and came back holding a first-aid kit. He tore the bottom of my pants and began pouring peroxide on the open womb. Once it cooled down, he began wrapping it with gauze until it was tight and secure.

"We gotta get you to a hospital," Big Nose Mike said in a panic.

"I'm good. I ain't going to no hospital. Just take me to Jami's."

"Man, you gotta get that shit checked out."

"I'm good, nigga. And I don't feel like being questioned. I just need some pain pills." I frowned because my shit was burning badly.

"I got a couple Percs," the other homie, JR, said and ran out to, I assumed, his car. When he came back, he handed me a few pills, and they carried me to the car.

I knew the pills would kick in soon. I just hoped I made it to Jami's before. I lay my head back on the seat, and Ru crossed my mind. He still hadn't called back, and the shit was sickening. I couldn't depend on the nigga fa shit. Like, damn, nigga. You ain't roll over once to pee and think about yo' bitch? I guess not. I shook my head as a sharp pain ran through my body. I couldn't wait until the meds kicked in, and I damn sure couldn't wait to get in a warm house.

Chapter 7 Chaotic

Trial Day Seven

S itting on the side of my attorney, I scanned the jurors who watched the DA make up a case. There were two Asians, one Black, and the rest Caucasian. I knew they were all judging me, not only because of my criminal history, but because of my tattoos. It was crazy how my life was in their hands no matter how innocent or guilty I was.

Everything the DA said, they wrote down and looked in my direction. The worst part was the picture of the little boy dead on the projector picture. They did this so the jurors would show no remorse for me and sympathy for the child. One thing I wouldn't do was let them see me sweat. I held my head high and challenged everyone in the courtroom with my eyes.

I even had the judge under pressure. I made sure to look him in his eyes anytime he looked in my direction. One thing I could say was, he was fair. The DA constantly tried to bring up old shit from my past, and the judge would shut him down each time. He didn't want it in his courtroom, and each time, he checked the fuck out of the DA.

"Your Honor, I would like to call my first witness."

"Okay. Now is your other witness here also? We have to get this trial going. We have two witnesses, no weapon, and nothing that has put Mr. Betterman at the scene except Mr. Frank."

"Yes, she's here." The DA looked back, and the second witness was sitting in the audience.

I looked back, and she looked at me as if she was puzzled it was me. She was a Hispanic lady who looked about her late thirties or early forties.

I looked over to the side just as Tuck was being escorted into the courtroom. I chuckled and sat back in my seat because this shit was about to get interesting. Tuck took the stand, and I could tell he was nervous. The clerk swore him in, and I watched as they began to ask him questions about the murder.

"So the night of the murder, where were you?" my attorney asked.

"Home, with my girl."

"Home, with your girl?" She began writing some things down, then looked back up at him. "In the first report, you told the detectives you were in the park."

"I was home with my girl, then left for the park."

"So you weren't there when it happened?"

"No, ma'am."

"So when you got to the park, what happened?"

"Umm...ummm... he walked up and said I just shot a kid."

"He, as in my client?"

"Yeaaa...yea...yes."

"And who was all there when Mr. Betterman said that he killed a kid?"

"Just him and I."

"Just you and him?" my attorney began writing again. "In the first statement, you mentioned, 'you and the homies.' So was it 'you and the homies' or just you and my client?"

The jurors began writing, and I could see they were in tune with that nigga's lies.

"Object, Your Honor?" The DA stood up.

"What are you objecting to?" the judge asked.

"She's badgering my witness."

"Overruled. Continue." He nodded to my attorney, and she smiled.

"It was uhh...just me and Chaotic."

"Okay, so after he mentioned killing the kid, what happened?"

"He said he was going home to his girl. He got in his car and left."

"His girl? And do you know who this girl is?"

"Nah."

"So you don't know his girl?" she asked again and pulled out another paper.

"Ha! Lying ass."

I turned around to my mother's voice.

The female bailiff walked over and said something to her, and she was still talking shit. My mother pulled everyone's attention, and when the courtroom finally settled, we continued.

"So his girlfriend isn't Mercedes Frank? Your cousin." She smirked, and Tuck's eyes grew wide.

He was caught in another lie, and this shit was comical. I sat back for the rest of his testimony and laughed. By the time my attorney was done with this nigga, he damn near had tears in his eyes. The bailiff, who had been dozing off the entire time, was wide awake and even laughed a few times. Tuck kept asking the judge if he could leave, and when he was done, the judge ordered him to stay. He made him sit right in front of the courtroom, and this gave me a chance to taunt him.

The DA called his next witness, and for some reason, she looked at Tuck hard, who was now seated in the first row. She took the stand, and the clerk swore her in.

"Thank you, Mrs. Gomez." The DA smiled at her, trying to get on her good side. "Mrs. Gomez, the night of the murder, where were you?"

"I was driving by."

"You were driving by the crime scene?"

"Jes," she pronounced with a J instead of a Y.

"Okay, and while you were passing by, had the police or paramedics arrived?"

"No. I drive by when the shooting happen."

"You drove by while the shooting was happening?"

"Jes."

"And what happened?"

"I see a little boy get shot. The guy driving drive off, so I follow."

"Did you get a chance to see the driver?"

"Jes."

"And in this courtroom, can you identify the driver as Mr. Betterman?"

"Objection, Your Honor. He's guiding the witness." My attorney jumped to her feet.

"Sustained."

"Mrs. Gomez, can you point to the person you saw driving the vehicle?"

"Jes. It was 'dat guy," she replied in her broken English and pointed past me.

The entire courtroom looked in the direction she was pointing, and I laughed. She pointed right at the nigga, Tuck, who was, in fact, the shooter that night. I couldn't say shit because for the millionth time, I wasn't a rat. This entire time, I was tripping off him making me the shooter when that nigga was the one that killed Amor's little brother all along. I wasn't nowhere on the scene, and this bitch ass nigga was tryna end my life all because he feared me.

"Mr. Frank, stand," the judge told him, nearly shaking his head. "Mrs. Gomez, is that who you pointed to as the suspect?"

"Jes. I saw him good. I remember him."

"Your Honor, my witness couldn't have been there. He was home with his girlfriend."

"I object!" Again, my attorney jumped to her feet in a rage.

"Sustained."

"Mrs. Gomez, did you see this man in the car?" The judge pointed to me.

She looked at me steadily and shook her head *no*. "No, sir. I see him, and a light-skinned boy with curly hair. I have the license plate. I wrote down," the lady replied, and she looked confident.

I sat back in my seat for the last time because this case was over. I smiled inside because all I could think of was getting home to Amor. If she had the plate number, the car they used was Tuck's baby mama, so definitely, it would lead back to him.

Everything that happened today was all God's work. I knew after this, shit was a wrap. The way the jurors looked and began writing on their pads, this case was over. *I'mma get my bitch*, I thought sitting back like a king. I looked back at my moms and winked. When she smiled, that shit made me feel better. My attorney was smiling, and the judge was frustrated with the whole case. I looked up to the air and thanked God, then focused my attention back on the judge.

❤️☐☐☐

Ecstatic about everything that had taken place in the courtroom, all I wanted to do was hear Amor's voice. Tuck was held in custody, and by the way my attorney was smiling, I knew I was gon' beat this shit. I was escorted to the back, and shortly after, my attorney came to holla at me. She was smiling from ear to ear, and that made me feel better.

"Mr. Betterman, this was one helluva day. Can you believe that asshole sat in this courtroom and was the suspect the whole time?" she asked, flabbergasted.

"Nah, that shit was wild," I replied, because I still wasn't gonna tell her I knew all along.

"Okay, so here it is. We can definitely get this case dropped, but the DA is still on his bull crap. Are you willing to take the case for the firearms found in your home?"

"Hell yeah."

"Okay, great." She released a breath of air I could tell she had been holding in. "That damn Mercedes Frank. Had she taken the case, all she would've gotten was maybe probation. Oh, well. Moving on."

"So what I'm looking at with that?"

"Four with half." She shrugged, uncertain.

"A'ight, fuck it," I agreed because four years with half sounded better than life.

She wrote some shit down and left excited. I headed to the phone, and before I dialed Amor, I called Lady Chaotic. She accepted the call, and the moment it went through, she began screaming.

"Bigggggg!"

I laughed. Because right now, I had a lot to smile about. "What's up, lady?"

"I miss you, nigga."

"I miss y'all too. What y'all doing? Where bro at?"

"That nigga went to make a sale. He be right back."

"A'ight. A'ight."

"What happened in trial today?" she asked because my attorney thought it was best her and my bro didn't come to court.

"That shit over. Mexican lady who was the witness said that nigga was the shooter."

"For real!" she screamed into the phone. We couldn't say

much over the phone, so Lady was gon' fake the fonk. She already knew Tuck was the shooter just as the whole hood. "So what now?"

"They want me to take the guns they found in the crib. Other than that, I'm coming home to get my bitch." I smiled and brushed the small goatee on my chin. The phone went silent for a moment, then I heard lady's voice.

"She got shot."

"Who got shot?"

"Lady Ru." She used Amor's hood name, and my heart dropped.

"She straight?"

"Yeah, she good. I talked to her on Facebook."

"Who was it?" I had to ask.

I prayed it wasn't one of my homies because I didn't want to have to kill one of my niggas for that girl.

"The mex," she said, and I nodded.

"Call her."

"Okay. Hold on." Lady clicked over, and after about a minute, she clicked back on the line.

"Lady Ru."

"Hey, Lady." I heard Amor's voice.

I paused for a minute because I was overwhelmed. "Amor, a nigga coming home, ma."

"What that mean?"

"It means, they got yo' lil' bro's killer. I told you it wasn't me, baby girl. But, check it. What's up with you getting shot?"

She paused, and I gave her ass some time to get her lie straight. "Yeah, it happened so fast," she replied sadly, and that shit pissed me off more.

"So you know what's finna happen, right?"

"Chaotic, please. It's handled."

"Ain't shit handled until I handle it." I shook my head. I meant what the fuck I said, and niggas was gon' die. I knew for Amor, niggas was gon' ride, but that wasn't enough for me. "Look, put some more minutes on yo' phone. I'mma have to go up north to reception for ninety days. I ain't gon' be able to call, but when I get my first call, I don't give a fuck if you with yo' nigga. You betta answer. Lady, I'm gone. I love you."

"Okay. Love you too, Big."

I hung up and headed for my bunk. This was a long day, and a nigga needed to rest. I had a clear head and a hard dick. In about twenty months, I was gonna feel that good ass pussy again. I couldn't wait.

Chapter 8 Amor

After hanging up with Chaotic, my heart was pumping. I sat in one spot in a complete zone. Right now, I ain't know how to feel. I mean, I was happy to know he wasn't responsible for my little brother's murder, but now what?

I knew the ninety days I wouldn't be able to talk to him would drive me crazy because I needed more information. Aside from my brother, I hated the fact he knew I had gotten shot. I knew how Chaotic was, and the exact reaction I got was exactly what I expected. No matter how much I said it was handled, he wasn't gon' give a fuck. My homies had bodies dropping, but I knew Chaotic was gon' paint the city red. That nigga didn't play when it came to me, and although it felt great to have someone love me so much, I still wanted him out of harm's way.

The night I got shot, I didn't hear from Ru until three p.m. that afternoon. By that time, I was so over it, and it only showed me I couldn't count on him. He picked me up from Jami's, and since we been home, he'd been tryna be at my beck and call, but it was too late.

I got up from the bed and leaped on one leg toward the living room. When I saw that Ru was screaming at the game, and I could hear a group of niggas talking to him, I knew he wasn't moving anytime soon.

"You need something?" He finally looked over and asked.

"I'm good."

I leaped past him and into the kitchen to grab a can of Pepsi. When I went back into my room, I settled in the bed, kicked my leg up, and called Rawdy.

"'Sup, homegirl? You straight?"

"Yeah, I'm great actually."

"How's your leg?"

"Good. What you doing?"

"Shit, on the block. I'm 'bout to hop in this dice game. See if I can win some of these niggas' money."

"Okay, well, I ain't gon' hold you, but ol' boy called. He said they got the nigga who did it."

"Word? Man, I told you. So is they gon' let him out?"

"Well, he took a gun case for some straps they found in his house. He's gonna call me in ninety days." I paused, wondering what she would say.

"You can write him, though."

"Yeah, I thought of that. So you not mad?"

"You want me to be honest?"

"Yes."

"Well, at first, when I was hearing y'all was on some creep shit, yes. I was really mad because despite you being my HG, you my friend, and I only got two of those. You kept it from me."

"I know, and I'm sorry. I just know how you feel about the Trey Nines."

"You right, but you my friend. All I can do is respect yo' wishes. After the night you were about to go to war for him with Boss, that told me you loved him. Not only that, but the way he stood up for you told me he loved you too, and one thing I can't do is stand between love. Lady Ru, follow yo' heart, ma."

"Awww, thanks, friend," I replied and paused for a moment. "I love him, Rawdy. I really don't know what to do from this point."

"Ru the homie, but like I said, you my friend, and you deserve to be happy. I watched you for years being good to that nigga. You tried and tried, and if he couldn't see it, he didn't deserve it. The heart wants what the heart wants. Always remember, what's one man's trash is another man's forever."

"One hunnit."

"I'mma get in this game. You get better because we miss yo' ass."

"Okay. Love you, HG."

"Love you too."

We disconnected, and I couldn't help but smile. It felt great to hear those words come from Rawdy because she hated them niggas. This let me know that she put my heart and what I desired before this hood shit, and that meant a lot to me. I didn't expect anyone else to understand. As long as Rawdy and Misha were on board, then I was happy.

Since Ru was busy, I took this as my chance to write Chaotic a letter. I knew after he received his time, he would leave to catch the chain up state in about two weeks after, so I was gonna stash it until I had a final address.

After writing Chaotic a short letter, I lay back on my bed and got lost in my thoughts. I couldn't wait until his address popped up in the system, so I could send my letter. I was curious about what return address I would use, but fuck it. I was gonna let him write me here at home. Ru never checked the mail because the only thing that came for him was the cable bill that he paid.

> *I love to see you walk into the room*
> *Body shining, lightin' up the place*
> *And when you talk, everybody stop*
> *'Cause they know you know just what to say, and*
> *The way that you protect your friends*
> *Baby, I respect you for that*
> *And when you grow, you take everyone you love along*
> *I love that shit!*

Chapter 9 Chaotic

Three Weeks Later

"Mail call!"

I heard one of the CO's yell out, and moments later, a letter slid under my cell. At first, I was kinda puzzled because it wasn't no telling who it could be. In situations like these, there were bitches who either gave up because they couldn't stay down, or there were bitches who felt because a nigga was in this situation he was vulnerable.

I picked the letter up, and when I saw Gutta Baby on the envelope, I smiled. I studied it long and hard with my heart racing.

Before I tore it open, I laughed because she was a bold muthafucka. She wrote me from her new address, and when I wrote her back, I was sending my letter right there.

To: Big Poppa (Chaotic)
From: Gutta Baby
Date: May, 8th 2019
Time: 2:34pm
Dedication: Beyonce "Hello"

Dear Chaotic,

First I wanna start by saying, I'm sorry. I'm sorry for so many reasons so first, for wrongfully accusing you of my brothers murder. Secondly, you having to find out I got shot. I know how you are so if I could have taken that to the grave I would. I know you won't let it go just please be safe. Anyway, I hope by the time this letter gets to you, you're in the best of spirits. I'm glad all of this is over now I could be at ease. My mind, my heart and my soul. Canyon, I would have literally died if you were found guilty. I can't front, I really was unsure and you can't blame me. You know just like I know. So again I'm happy this is all over and we could continue where we left off. Speaking of, that last night spent with you was blissful. Everything was so perfect and just being in your arms was heart feeling. You made me feel secure in your arms and I never wanted the night to end. I'm still curious about your intentions that morning. Like what were you gonna do? I mean you pretty much strong armed me. Lol. I know things between us were demented but in my heart we were destined. God made all this happen and I'm sure it's because we both deserve genuine love. For some reason, I feel genuinely loved by you and you got the same from me. I've never felt like this about no nigga. I'm not gonna go into much detail until you respond. By then I'll know if you received this and we can go from there.

As I read the letter, the entire time, I smiled gleefully. It was like Amor knew all the right shit to say, and she got straight to the point. When she said we were destined, it went perfectly with the way I felt, but when she said God made it happen because we both deserved genuine love, a nigga's heart skipped a few beats. It was definitely God's work, and I'd forever be in debt. I wasn't a spiritual nigga, but I did believe in God. Every day before court, I dropped to my knees and prayed He'd get me home to that girl. My prayers were answered, and to have her back in my good graces meant a lot to me.

All I ever wanted was a down bitch. One I could rely on when shit in them streets got heavy, and one who would hold my best interest at heart. If I could get Amor with no baggage, I swear, on my pops, I was gon' do right by her. I was gonna give her the love she deserved and stay solid for the rest of our eternity.

I remembered everything she said about her relationship with Ruger the night we were on the beach and how he treated her. So most definitely, I didn't come into her life to play. I knew she needed me, not for sex, but to repair her and remind her of her worth.

After reading Amor's letter, I pulled out the paper and pen one of my homies gave me when I first arrived. I took a seat at my desk and began writing a response letter. I couldn't put my full emotions into it; I was gonna save that until after my most valued question.

Once I was done writing, I lay on my bed and put on my headphones. I went to my NBA YoungBoy *Never Broke Again* album and pushed play on my fav song from the CD.

Just give me a chance, promise I'mma make you love me

And Me and you together could accomplish more than something

Askin' would I leave, baby that's outta the question

Everything I make a day, I bring it back you count it for me

Ummmm, right or wrong

I'll never salt you down

I hope you feel me through this song

Promise you won't never leave me 'lone

Chapter 10 Amor

To: My Gutta Baby

From: Your Poppa

Date: May, 29th 2019

Time: I don't even know

Dear Amor,   Dedication: Webbie "Gutta Bitch"

Let's get this out the way first.... Yo ass hanging
out and you know a nigga don't like this shit but
Ima let it slide (for now). Amor I miss the fuck
outta you ma. I understand how you felt and
knowing our hoods are enemies I expect it. It feels
good to know you smiling. It feels good to know
this shit over with because the worst part of it all
was hurting you. I know you had doubts and now
you know the real. Look I ain't come into yo life to
play games. From the jump I knew I wanted you
and I saw a future with you. Man you don't know
how good it felt to see this letter slid under my
door. Oh and I see yo thirsty ass found me. Lol jk.

My thirsty ass was smiling from ear to ear like "Look At Her"
you ain't give me a chance to get processed in. Lol. You did
that. Anyway, I heard you moved and shit. I ain't gone lie that
shit crushed me. I'm like damn my bitch gone to be happy wit
her nigga. :(Speaking of, my intentions that day were to
make you mine. Ma, you wasn't going back to that house. You
was gone be staying at my moms until I got us another crib.
That nigga lucky. After that good pussy you really think I
was letting you go? Nahhh. Right now, we got a little bump in
the road but in due time I'm coming back for you. What's up
you ready to be mine or you gone stay with that nigga? If so, I
respect it. I'm not gone go further until I know. Oh and I see
you wrote from your home. Slick Ass.

Wit Love,
Yo Poppa!

Over the last few weeks, Chaotic and I had been writing back and forth. I received a letter every three days, and I wrote him back each time. He was finally transferred to a prison that was only an hour away from where I lived. He sent a visiting form that I was eager as hell to fill out and send in to be approved. I was definitely sending it soon, and I couldn't wait to see him.

I folded up the letter and the form because after sitting on the toilet in my restroom for nearly an hour, I knew Ru would come looking for me soon. Therefore, I had to regroup because the entire time I read Chaotic's letter, the nigga had me smitten. I couldn't wait to write him back and answer the question about me being his girl. That was the part that had me smiling so hard my jaws hurt. I was unsure of how I would pull it off because of my situation with Ru, but for him, I was gonna try. It was crazy because one thing I wasn't was a cheater, but this man had me ready to throw it all away. It was like I was confident knowing Chaotic loved me.

Right now, I couldn't write back because Ru was in and out of the bedroom, so I was gonna wait until he left tomorrow to go to the hood. I noticed since I was on bed rest he had been using this as his chance to leave more, and I didn't care. I needed that energy away from me; I just prayed he would be okay. No matter how much Ru and I's relationship had fallen apart, I always said a prayer for him because it would hurt me if something ever happened to him. Not only me, but Heaven, because she loved her father to death.

Knock! knock! knock!

I quickly stuffed the papers into my purse before responding to Ru's knocks.

"I'm coming out now." I got up from the toilet and ran some water to look like I washed my hands.

"What's up? What you doing?"

"Nothing, I was using it," I lied.

"Nah, like, what you about to do?"

"Just work on the boutique."

"Cool. Can I lay with you?" he asked, shocking the hell out of me.

"Sure. I guess." I shrugged and hopped over to my bed.

I dropped my purse on the side of me, then grabbed my computer. Ru helped me get into bed and get comfy before lying down next to me.

"What you got new you working on?" he asked, acting interested in my work.

"Well, I'm designing pieces myself now. Heaven Couture instead of the normal wholesale items I always buy. I'm tryna brand myself with my own original fabrics."

"That's what's up. Heaven Couture, that's dope, yo." He smiled and began scrolling on his phone.

"I wanna open a storefront," I mumbled off but Ru wasn't paying me any attention. Instead of repeating myself, I decided to just move on. "Ru, I'm thinking about getting a boat."

"A boat? And do what?"

"Really? You know I love the ocean. I don't know. I just think I could get more done with a clear mind. I wanna live on it three days a week, sail out, sketch designs, and even catch fish to eat." I giggled because I knew it sounded crazy.

"That's dope. You should do it."

"You'll let me?" I smiled excitedly, although the nigga didn't include himself.

I mean, what nigga in their right mind would let their woman live apart from them three days a week? Not to mention, out in the ocean. A nigga who don't give a fuck, that was who. Granted, I was excited, but I did make a mental note of how easy it was for him to agree.

"Yeah, if that's what you wanna do."

"It's a dream." I faintly smiled—in my feelings a little.

"What's up? Let me get some." He tugged at my shorts.

"I knew you wanted something, nigga." I rolled my eyes at his ass.

"It's been weeks. I need to let my rocks off." He tried to plead as he tugged his sack.

I let out a soft sigh and told him to come on. This was still a part of my duty, so I agreed.

❤️🔲🔲

It was the second week since I sent in the visiting form, so I was eager to get to my mailbox. I headed out my door and across the street to the mail boxes. Because we lived in the desert, the mailboxes were about a mile apart. Just my luck, the house I moved in had a box directly across the street. I stuck my key inside, and when I saw the tons of pieces of mail, I got excited. I skimmed through, and there was a card from Chaotic, and the response from visiting. I locked my box and quickly headed into the house. Ru was in the hood, and Heaven had just gone to sleep, so it was just me and my thoughts. I tore into the response letter and began reading.

NOTICE OF VISITOR DISAPPROVAL
VISITOR COPY

Inmate: Betterman, Canyon

Barkley, Amor   *6/10/2019*

You are disapproved to visit based on one or more reasons as stated per California Code of Regulations (CCR), Title 15, Section 3172.1. Approval/Disapproval of Prospective Visitors and/or Section 3176.3, Exclusion of a Person from Institution/Facilities. The specific reason(s) for your disapproval is indicated below.

3172.145.3 (b)(6)(A) - You have omitted: LIST OF FULL CRIME HISTORY

Send the omitted information with a copy of this notice directly to Visitor Processing.

After reading the disapproval letter, my heart set in the bottom of my shoe. My little feelings were so hurt I read the letter over and over hoping they made a mistake. Basically, they wanted me to list everything on my criminal history that I failed to mention. The last case I caught was two firearms, and that was exactly what I had put. I was done with the probation and the joint suspension, so I wasn't sure what they expected aside from that.

Determined to see this man, I grabbed my daughter and bundled her up into her car seat. She was still asleep, so I ran into the kitchen to make her a cup, then flew out the door to the DOJ office. After strapping Heaven into her seat, I looked in my purse to make sure I had three forms of ID, so I could do my fingerprinting and they could send me my criminal print out.

Just as we were pulling out of my driveway, my phone began to ring, and it was Chaotic. I knew he was gonna be upset, so I was nervous as hell.

"'Sup, ma?" His sexy ass voice blessed the phone, and I couldn't help but smile.

"Hey, babe," I cooed into the phone, and I could hear the smile on his face.

"Loving you, missing you. I got some bad news." There was a sudden mood change, and I already knew what it was.

"I already know."

"Oh, you got the disapproval letter?"

"Yes, it came today. I'm on my way down to the DOJ office to get my criminal print out, so I can resend the visiting form."

"Damn, you on it, huh?" He chuckled, taunting me.

"Hell yeah. I need to see you." I smiled bashfully into the phone.

"Man, who you telling? A nigga missing you bad, Cute Face."

Again, I smiled because, with all the nicknames this man had for me, *Cute Face* stood out the most.

"Aww, baby."

"You get your card?"

"Yeah, I got it. Thank you."

"You welcome. Where the baby?"

"She's right here with me." I looked through my rearview at a sleeping Heaven. "Canyon, are you gonna write tonight?"

"I really don't be writing when I'm in prison, but for you, I got you. And I ain't wanna get you in trouble sending mail to yo' crib."

"Fuck all that, babe. Can you just start writing me more?"

"Yep. Write me tonight, and I'mma respond."

"Okay."

"So you straight? You need anything? The baby need anything?"

"Canyon, noooo. We good. Do you need anything?"

"I'm straight. As long as y'all straight, I'm straight."

"Awww, I love you for it too." I smiled warmly.

No matter what, every time I talked to Canyon, he'd ask if Heaven and I were okay. That shit always made me feel good because her dad would never ask were we okay and if we needed things. Ru always felt like I had it and it was under control. He depended on me, and sometimes, I struggled. I mean, I made great money with my boutique, but the money wasn't coming as fast as it was when I was husting.

Shit was hard now, and Ru didn't understand it. He was still hustling his weed, but I didn't get a dime of that money. He let me pay for every date, whenever we went out to eat, and even our daily turn ups. He paid a couple bills, which were very helpful, but seventy-five percent of our cost of living was on me.

"I'm 'bout to get back in this line. I love you, ma. I'll call you as soon as it's my turn again."

"Okay. I love you too."

He blew a kiss into the phone, and I replied with a juicy ass kiss. We disconnected, and about another five minutes later, I pulled into my destination. I was determined to see this man, so I said a short prayer before getting out of my car.

Chapter 11 Chaotic

To: Big Poppa (Chaotic)
From: Gutta Baby
Date: June 14th, 2019
Time 11:26pm
Dedication: Tamia "Officially Missing You"

Dear Chaotic,

Ima start this letter off by saying "I Miss You" I lay
around with so many thoughts, and tears in my eyes
because of how much I not only miss you but need you. I
find it strange how a man could come into my life and
shake things up the way you've done. What's really
crazy is we've never been together and it feels like I've
been your wife for years. I can't do as much right now to
show you I'm down for you but I'm here and I'll do my
best. I swear you use to drive me crazy when you were
out. Those pop ups, and quick visits always made me feel
like you really didn't want me but then when I thought
about it, only someone interested would take time out of
their day to check up on someone. Oh yeah and sorry for
the Monster I threw on you Lol. Can I be honest? I
used to be jealous when you would post your girlfriend. I
wasn't jealous of her, I was jealous she had you. Nobody
in the world deserves you Canyon but me.

Chaotic, Chaotic, Chaotic, boy what are you doing to me? Or should I say what did you do to me because it's done. I'm already gone off you. I used to pray you would do something to turn me off so I can leave your ass alone but you didn't; you were perfect. Smh. Now look at me. Everything about you won me over and when you put that dick on me, that shit blew me back. Although we had that rocky start, I thought of that night everyday. I don't wanna say this is all made up because I have faith in us. Please don't let me down because I know how this jail shit go. Off that! I can't wait until you come home. All I wanna do is lay in your arms, while you hold me tight. I wanna talk to you about everything from my past, my childhood, shit other than the stupid gangbanging. I also wanna know everything about you so if you can please answer these questions. I know this may be corny but I believe when you like someone you're supposed to know everything about them.

Here we go...

1. What's your favorite food?
Seafood
2. What's your favorite movie?
Pretty Woman
3. What's your favorite R&B song?
Ashanti Baby
4. What's your favorite Oldie?
Isley Brothers (Don't Say Goodnight)
5. If there was one place in the world you could go where would it be?
Outer Space
6. If you had a choice to be any superhero who would it be?
Mines would be Disney Princess (The Little Mermaid)
7. Who is your favorite person in the world other than your kids?
My Grandmother (Maria Amor Lopez)
8. What's one thing you enjoy doing?
Drawing
9. What's your favorite sexual position?
Doggy style Lol (embarrassed)
10. What's your favorite place in the world to have sex?
The Beach (wink)

Your turn...

Ps. I love you Chaotic! I love you more than you think, In my eyes your perfect and I wouldn't change a thing about you Poppa. (Muahhhh)

Sincerely Yours,
Gutta Baby, Cuteface, Your Ryda...AMOR

I laughed hard as fuck at Amor's letter because of the ending. Everything she said touched a nigga, but that damn ending was corny as hell. I couldn't front, though. She got me with those questions. The shit made me smile because no bitch had ever taken the time out to even ask. True, Amor knew a lot about me already, and I'd been noticed that, but these questions were kinda different. Just reading the part about my favorite sexual position had my dick hard as fuck. Then when I read her favorite place to fuck was the beach, I damn near nutted on myself.

Right now, all a nigga had was lustful memories, so I closed my eyes and lay my head back. Before I knew it, I had my dick in my hand stroking it to the memory of Amor's sweet, tight pussy. *Bend over*, I thought and visualized her tooting her fat ass in the air. I slid my dick into her, and before I began stroking her, I traced her back with kisses.

I couldn't wait until I got home because this was something I often visualized. I wanted to kiss Amor's entire body and tell her I loved her. *Damn*. I slid into her tight pussy and stroked her nice and long. I wanted to take my time with her because she was precious. I kept my eyes closed as I made love to an image of her still bent over while the waves were crashing. When I felt my nut coming, I began jacking my dick harder until I released all over my hand. There was so much cum coming out of me, I stroked it until I was done.

Once I got every drop out of me, I jumped down from my bed to grab my towel. I cleaned myself up and took a seat at my desk and read the letter once more. I was gonna write her back, but before I did, I opened the second envelope from the Warden that contained Amor's DOJ info. I began to read the long form, and the more I read, the more I got upset. The entire time, my blood was boiling, and I couldn't read anymore. I jumped to my feet and called for the CO so I could go out to make a call.

Watching Ms. Rodriguez walk down the tier, toward my cell, I shook my head. There were seven CO's on duty tonight, and this thirsty bitch had to be the one to come.

When she got to my cell, she smirked. "What's up, Better-man?"

"I need to make a call."

She paused, then reached for her keys to unlock my cell. I walked right past her ass and went straight to the phone. I swear that bitch was on my dick tough. So tough that everyone around me knew it. They often told me how crazy I was because I could use her to my advantage, but fuck that. I had a point to prove to Amor, so I was coming into her life with a clean slate.

"Amor!" I raged into the phone the moment she said hello after accepting the call.

"Dang, hi to you too."

"Man, don't 'hi' me. I'mma beat yo' ass, ma. The fuck is up with this shit from DOJ? Ma, yo' fucking rap sheet longer than mine. A fucking accessory to murder, are you fucking serious?"

"That's old, Canyon."

"I know its old, but what the fuck were you doing with your life? Ma, the shit go all the way back to a fucking grand theft when you were thirteen. Two fucking different gun cases, and a fucking murder." I shook my head as if she could see me.

She was quiet as hell because her ass couldn't defend herself. This shit was from the DOJ, so it was all true. I understood her life years ago and how she was so caught up in the streets, but I couldn't front. I was disappointed as fuck. Just the thought of her niggas letting her get into shit like that wasn't cool. I already didn't approve of the gang-banging, but this? I knew that accessory to murder was a nigga, and that shit really hurt me. I would kill the world if something happened to this girl, and seeing this shit had me on one.

"I'm sorry," she finally spoke in a low tone.

I continued shaking my head because that was all I could do. I waited for a brief moment and gathered myself before I replied. "It's nothing to be sorry about. I just hope you done because if something happens to you, I'll lose it."

"I'm done, Canyon."

"A'ight, ma. I'm still beating yo' ass. Give me a kiss."

"Muahhhh."

I could hear the juiciness from her lips, and it made my dick hard all over. "I'm 'bout to go write you back. I love yo' crazy ass. Don't forget what I said, ma. I'll lose it if something ever happened to you."

"Okay, and I love you too. You gon' call back?" she asked, and I could tell she wanted to talk to me.

"Yes, Cute Face, I'mma call back. Give me about an hour,

a'ight?"

"Okay."

I hung up the phone and headed back into my cell. I took a seat at my desk and began replying to her letter. I stuffed the letter from the DOJ into my paperwork because I couldn't stomach looking at it. I was gonna focus on the letter and drop some jewels on baby. I couldn't wait until I got to the questions because we had so much in common.

Like seafood being her favorite because it was also mine too. I loved tacos, but crab legs were my number one go-to. The beach also. I loved the beach so much it was where I'd go after every lick I hit to get my thoughts together. I didn't know if it was because I was an Aquarius or what, but anything that had to do with water always pulled at my emotions. No matter if it was the beach, a lake, a pool, hell, even the shower. Whenever I had the chance, I'd take three showers a day. That was what I missed most about being free. A nigga was in this hell hole with barely-hot water and was told when to take showers.

I couldn't wait to go home. Especially because I had a new life waiting on me. Little did Amor know, I wasn't playing games because I would never make a fool out of her. Like I said, she was precious, so I was gonna treat her as such. With no regrets and no muthafucking scars.

Chapter 12 Amor

To: My Gutta Baby

From: Your Poppa

Date: 6/18/19

Time: Don't Know Ma

Dedication: Keith Sweat "Make It Last Forever"

Cute Face,

I see you just got this shit all figured out huh? So I'm the one you wanna spend your life with? I hope you sure about that. Lady Ru don't have me going crazy over you then switch up on me. Baby girl, you don't want them problems, trust me. Look I wasn't tryna run from you or no shit like that. I was just protecting my little heart; Gangstas got feelings too. I was avoiding being hurt and I was avoiding hurting you. You don't know how many nights I laid next to that girl thinking of you and knowing it was prolly killing you. Not only that, but I saw how you was moving and I wasnt tryna be another nigga on yo hit list. Lol. I can't front though, I been at ease since you came into my life. You brought a nigga a sense of peace I been searching for, for an eternity. Despite the shit we just went through I'm really at fucking peace with you. Who would have ever thought, one conversation of football would lead to my future. Damn. There's no turning back Amor we're all in. I love you and since nobody deserves me but you, Ima hold you to that.

1. My fav food..

Seafood

2. My fav movie

Belly

3. My fav R&B song

R Kelly "All I Really Want"

4. My fav oldie

Atlantic Starr "Am I Dreaming"

5. A chance to go anywhere in the world

Africa (and not because I watch too much Belly lol I've always wanted to go.

6. Super hero

Captain America

7. Fav person in the world

My Mother

8. What I enjoy doing

Listening to music

9. Fav position

You laying flat on your stomach

10. Fav place to fuck

The Beach (and since we both love the beach that's where we gone make our

daughter)

I love you to death with no scars cute face. I want you to tell me everything about you ma. Please don't hold nothing back. I'll never judge you.

After reading my baby's letter, I was all smiles. The other day, he tried to call and chew my ass out, but he let it go the moment he heard my voice. Got 'emmmm! No matter how tough he was, Chaotic was soft for me, and he showed me that a long time ago. I couldn't front; the shit was cute because it showed he really cared about me. It felt so damn good to have someone who genuinely cared.

I'd often feel like I was alone in this world. I knew I had my friends and my daughter, but friendships only went so far. Ru was the last person on Earth I felt cared about my well-being. I knew what everyone was thinking: why she still with the nigga? Keep shit real, at one point, I always banked on hope. Now it was contentedness. I wasn't in love with Ruger, I was content. The ideal of having a man around and to keep my daughter happy meant everything to me.

Often, I'd study Ru and ask myself why I was putting myself through it until I saw the way my daughter would light up when she saw her dad. I guess you can say I sacrificed my heart for my child. It was crazy how my physical love was there with Ruger, but my heart, body, and soul was on that penitentiary yard with Chaotic.

The more we talked, the more we wrote—the more we fell in love. I was beginning to feel guilty to the point I just wanted to end things with Ru because I couldn't stand to look at him knowing my heart was elsewhere.

(213) 599-4230: *Cute Face.*

I looked down at my phone and instantly began to smile. I studied the number for a brief moment, then texted back.

Me: *Baby? Who phone?*

(213) 599-4230: *It's mine, ma. I just bought it.*

Me: *Didn't we discuss this already? I told you no, not to get a damn phone.*

(213) 599-4230: *I'm sorry, baby girl, but I needed to talk to you.*

Me: *But what if you get caught? That's more time added to your time.*

(213) 599-4230: *Chill, ma. I'm good. Look, we only gon' talk on it at night. I'mma still use the wall phone during the day, and we gon' still write.*

Me: *A'ight, nigga.*

(213) 599-4230: *I love you, baby girl. I'm gonna put it up. I'mma hit you tonight.*

Me: *Okay.*

I replied with a sad face because out of all the days for him to get a cell phone, it had to be today. Today was Ru's birthday, and tonight, I had a surprise for him. He was currently in the room getting dressed while Jami was upstairs bathing all the kids. She had driven down to baby sit for us, and she brought her kids along. Her oldest daughter, Samira, loved her some Heaven, and Heaven loved that girl back. Therefore, I knew Heaven would be good while we were gone.

"Let's roll, Lady." Ru walked out the room smelling like Oud For Happiness.

I couldn't front; he made me stop and look in his direction. He was wearing all-black Armani that I had picked out. His locks were pinned back, and he wore every piece of jewelry he owned. In another lifetime, I would have been turned on, but not tonight. However, I was gon' be nice because this was his birthday.

Every year for Ru's birthday, I always did some nice and fly shit. For my birthday, I got flowers, Hennessy, and maybe a massage. The massages always ended with sex, and after the third massage, I learned this was his way of getting me. I knew tonight I was gon' have to bend this shit over for him, so I was gonna get drunk as hell. We headed out the house, and I seemed more excited than him. His energy wasn't off like normally, so I was cool.

"Where we going?" he asked the moment we were in the car.

"I don't know. Where you wanna go?"

"I don't know. Shit, out to eat or something?"

"Let's go eat on the beach."

"A'ight," he replied and headed for the highway.

The night air was perfect for the beach, and the Givenchy

71

dress I decided to wear was perfect. I kept it simple with some three-inch peep-toe heels that I was gonna remove to walk through the sand. My hair was bone-straight with a side part, so my bangs hung loosely in my face. Ru didn't know about the surprise, so I was gonna play dumb.

When we arrived, I instructed him to park. I told him let's get out and walk the boardwalk, and surprisingly, he agreed. We began walking the bicycle lane, and when we neared the spot my cousin had instructed me to come to, I tugged at his arm, and we headed that way. Because my leg had pretty much healed up, it was easy for me to get across the sand. So with excitement, I pulled Ru's arm.

"Man, my shoes 'bout to be fucked up."

"So what? We'll get more." I continued to pull him. "Ooh, what's that?" I asked with excitement because I could see the candles and lights from afar.

When we finally made it through the sand and got close to the surprise, Ru finally noticed what was going on and smiled. He looked at me, then looked around at the décor, and I could tell he was impressed. There was a table set up with nice decorations, candles, and bottles of liquor. My cousin lifted the food warmer, and inside was lobster, king crab, bacon-wrapped asparagus, and lobster mac n cheese. It was a cute little sign that read *Drink Up Beaches,* and everything was set up perfectly. I used my cousin, who was a *Bae Night* decorator @PicNicsOfPurpurse. Not only did she decorate for romantic events, but she cooked her ass off. She was the one who prepared the meal tonight, so it was a two birds with one stone type of thing. I got my girl @Citazdrinkzandthingz to blend us some drinks because she was a professional bartender, and everything turned out perfect.

"Aww, thanks, shorty." Ruger looked at me smiling hard.

Thanks shorty? I thought to myself. No hug, no kiss, no excitement. Damn, I felt that one, but I couldn't be mad.

"You're welcome." I smiled back and took a seat.

My cousin, Tasha, came over and began hosting. We made

small talk as Ru rolled a blunt and put flame to it. The entire time I looked out into the ocean, which was only a few feet away, and got lost in my thoughts. It made me think of the night Chaotic and I spent here. It was actually the same beach just a few miles down. I smiled at just the thought, and it was crazy because my phone began to vibrate right on cue. For some strange reason, I already knew it was Chaotic, so I looked up at Ru to see what he was doing. He was busy on his phone, so I began texting with Canyon.

After texting him a few more times, I didn't get a response, so I gave up. I put my phone into my purse, and again, I got lost in my thoughts. My cousin began serving us the food as Ru continued to smoke and toy around on his phone. We all began to make small talk, and once our plates set in front of us, we began diving in. Right after we ate, Ru poured us a glass of Hennessy, and in no time, I was good and drunk.

Everything around us was so calm and peaceful, and it gave me time to think. I looked at Ru a few times while my mind was on Chaotic heavy. I knew he was upset, and it began bothering me. I wanted so badly to text him again, but I didn't bother. I continued to watch Ru, and it was like my reality began setting in; it was over with us. As romantic as the scenery was, not once did he kiss me, grab my hand, walk the beach with me, nothing. It was like I was here with a friend.

That was exactly what Ru was, a friend. He was like the best friend I lived with and bore a child with. Ru was always by my side no matter what, but he wasn't emotionally invested in me. Just sitting here looking at the full moon made me realize the heart wanted what it wanted, and Ru's heart didn't yearn for me. Throughout it all, I was the one to blame. That man just wasn't into me, and I had to face reality.

"Let's have a threesome." I looked at Ru over the burning candles. I watched his face for a moment, and I could tell I caught him off guard.

He looked at me and chuckled. "Girl, shut yo' ass up."

"For real, Ru, let's do it."

"Yo' ass crazy. And who you supposed to be doing this with?"

"I don't know. I'll find somebody," I replied, and again, he laughed.

I couldn't even front if I wanted to. The shit hurt my feelings, and this told me right there it was really over. Once upon a time, Ru would die if I asked him something like this. He knew how I felt about sharing because when it came to my nigga, I was very territorial. I really didn't plan on a damn threesome. This was just another test that he failed. Instead of speaking on it further, I got quiet and hid back the tears threatening to fall. Never in my wildest years would I expect him to be so accepting about something like this. Granted, he didn't say yes, but I could see it all in his face, and the laughter that escaped his lips, he was whiling. All this did was help me make up my mind. I was gonna choose between my mind and heart, and Chaotic was where my heart belonged.

Chapter 13 Chaotic

A Few Weeks Later

"What's up, ma?"

"Hey, babe."

"What yo' ass doing?"

"Nothing, right here with the baby and doing some work."

"A'ight. Anything new with the boutique?"

"Yessss...oh my God, I have some new sketches. I also found a reasonable seamstress."

"Awe, that's what's up. I'm proud of you."

I smiled, really proud of baby girl. I loved the way she made shit happen when it came to her business. Amor was passionate as fuck about her craft, and I couldn't wait until I got out. I had plans of getting her a storefront because I heard her mention it plenty of times. Every time she mentioned it, I could hear the excitement in her voice, and that shit always made me feel good.

"Thank youuu."

"Can I ask you something?"

"Sure."

"Where the fuck yo' nigga at?"

"He's right here."

"Like, right there?"

"Not right *here*, but I'm looking dead at him. Why you ask?"

"Because I've been talking to you nonstop. Amor, you answer this phone every time I call, ma, and I ain't never heard cuz say two words to you."

"Yeah, well."

"Is this how you been living?"

"Yes," she replied sadly, and I shook my head.

"That's crazy. You know I don't be in yo' business, but I remember always watching yo' snaps, and the nigga was never around. You used to be all over the house cooking and doing all types of shit, and I never saw him in yo' background."

"He doesn't bother me, I guess."

"Bother you? You his bitch. He supposed to bother you. Why you stay so long?"

"I don't know, Canyon. The baby I guess."

"Yeah, well, I know yo' little mama needs him, so keep him around until I get out. I got it from there."

"Honestly, he prolly won't be around too long. After the night on the beach, I made up my mind. I asked him for a threesome, and he basically agreed. Not only that, but that night gave me time to think, and the nigga just ain't in love with me. I'm the one to blame."

"The nigga agreed to a threesome?" I fumed.

"Yeah. I'm not doing it. I just wanted to see where his head was at."

"That's crazy as fuck," I spoke into the phone, not believing my ears. One thing I wasn't into was threesomes because I didn't give a fuck; a nigga or bitch wasn't touching mines. Often, women used sleeping with another woman as an excuse to sleep around, but in my eyes, it was still cheating. "You made yo' appointment to come up here?" I changed the subject and got excited. She had finally gotten approved to come visit, and I couldn't wait to see her.

"Yes. It's Sunday at nine a.m."

"Damn, I can't wait to see yo' ass."

"I know. I'm excited and nervous."

"Why you nervous?"

"I don't know. Shit, it's been over a year since I last saw you, and when you were out, I wasn't yo' girl."

"You right, but don't be nervous, ma," I replied and smiled.

We continued to talk for a while, then I told her I was gonna hit her back. I needed to hit the yard because a nigga owed me some money.

Since the day I stepped foot on this yard, I had the work sewed up. One of my homies had his girl bring it in at visiting, and we were making a killing. I really ain't do as much as I could've, but I did what needed to be done to help Amor. I understood her situation with her nigga, and the nigga had gotten too comfortable. Despite him living there, her bills still needed to be paid, and the constant flowers kept a smile on her face. I really ain't tell her what I was up to because I knew she would trip, however, she knew I was doing something because the money stayed rolling in.

"Canyon Betterman!" I heard my name being called over the loudspeaker, so I got up from my seat and headed for the gates.

I had my Levis creased up, and a fresh pair of these fake chucks they gave us. Last night, I had my Hispanic homie cut my hair, so a nigga was feeling fresh. When the CO opened the gate, I walked out the building and headed for the visiting room. After handing a CO my prison ID, he pointed toward the room where they held the visits. When I walked through the door, Amor was sitting at table number forty-one with her head down. I stopped for a brief moment and took in her appearance. Even in the bull-shit clothing they made you wear, she was still looking good. When she finally looked up at me, a wide smile spread across her face, and she stood to her feet. I strolled over to her and took her into my arms for a hug. I then grabbed her face and kissed her until the CO told us to have a seat.

"What's up, Cute Face?" I reached across the table and grabbed her hands. I could tell she was nervous because all she did was smile and wouldn't make eye contact with me. "Dang, I finally got to see you."

She squeezed my hand and looked me in the eyes. A tear fell from her eye, so I reached over to wipe it away.

"It's my allergies," she tried to lie.

"Allergies, my ass." We both laughed, and a few more tears fell from her face. "Damn, you really love a nigga, huh?"

"Yes, I love you."

"I love you too. Damn, a nigga miss the fuck outta you."

"I miss you too," she faintly replied and looked at me. For some reason, I felt her energy, and I knew what was next. "What happened?" she spoke lowly, and my heart began to race.

"Let's go walk," I told her, and we stood up from the table.

I grabbed her hand, and we headed outside. We began walking the small yard, and I told her everything from the day it happened until the day in trial. By the time I was done, she was crying and told me sorry over and over for accusing me. I consoled her as I told her she had all rights. I let out a deep sigh because I had finally gotten it off my chest. I knew this day would come, and I owed her that.

I took her by the hand again and led her back inside to our

table. She grabbed the small clear bag that had single dollar bills, and we headed for the vending machine. After purchasing rotisserie chicken, fried rice, a cheese burger, and a couple of sodas, we headed back over to our table and began eating. She had finally loosened up, so we began to talk about all types of shit. It was like everyone around was invisible, and everything in our lives didn't matter. We laughed, we held hands, and we finally embraced as a couple.

Before our visit was over, we went to the photo booth and took three pictures. Because I didn't want her getting caught up at home, I kept the photos with me. When it was time for her to leave, my entire mood changed because I ain't want her to go. Already, I couldn't wait until the weekend for our next visit that she promised she wouldn't miss. Just watching Amor walk through the gates had a nigga's heart racing. I knew I loved this girl because she was still in my eyesight, and I missed her already.

"Betterman."

My name was called, and it broke me from my daze. I grabbed my ID and followed the CO back to my building, along with the other inmates. I couldn't wait to get back into my cell because I was gonna call and talk to her on her ride home.

Chapter 14 Amor

Amorrrr tell him you love me!

Canyon

Stop playing with him

Plz just give me some time

Plzzzz babe

Okay

Don't do this

Okay

I'm sorry

FUCC cuzz

♥ ♥ 🏁 🍶 >

OnG

Man I'm not sharing you with no
Nigga OnG

You my bitch

All these nigga failed

LOVE YOU MA' ♥ ♥ ♥

But your confusing me

Oh I know

One min u ain't tripping next u
are

Ain't no confusion

I'm tripping in a few months

📷 Ⓐ Text Message ⬆

After going back and forth with Chaotic, I was stressed the fuck out. One minute, he wasn't tripping off Ru. Then the next, he was demanding I tell him about us. I understood where he was coming from, but it wasn't as easy as it seemed. Yes, my heart was with him, and no, I didn't love Ru, but there was a child involved.

I knew I couldn't use Heaven as my excuse to stay because I knew I needed to let go and be happy. However, it wasn't that damn easy.

Over the course of a couple months, everything with Chaotic and I began blossoming. We had regular weekly visits and talked on the phone all day. If we weren't talking, we were texting. Meanwhile, Ru had no knowledge of it because he ain't pay me any attention. It was like since the candlelight beach dinner, things had changed drastically. They were worse than before, and it really felt like I had a damn roommate. A few times, he brought up the threesome, and even one time, when I stayed over Jami's, he called nonstop. I guess he was waiting on his invite over assuming we would use her. I really didn't play too much into it because like I said, it was a test.

The way Chaotic had begun to act, I knew my time was ticking, and I needed to move fast. I contemplated doing the threesome and ending things with Ruger, but Chaotic would literally die. Countless times, I've thought of ways to end things with Ru, but I couldn't figure out a way. I even thought of the old text trick, but that was played out. Therefore, I decided to go snooping on his social media, something I never did. At one point, I lived for checking his phone and hacking his accounts, but as time went by, the love began to fade, and so did my desire for catching him cheating. It was like I didn't care enough to care.

I went to my Facebook app and logged out. I entered Ru's email, then the passcode I knew he used. Ruger was one of those simple minded niggas who would use the same passcode for everything and never changed it. After entering the passcode, I was in and went straight to his inbox. I skimmed through a few bullshit messages, but when I got to the name Tina, I stopped. I began reading their messages, and at first, it was nothing. Ru even told her he had a family and even sent the link to my boutique trying to promote me to her. I continued to read, and baby girl wasn't giving up.

That was when things got juicy. They began flirting, and he

told her to send him a picture. Instead of a picture, she sent a video playing with her pussy. When I say my mouth literally hit the floor? I was stuck. I mean, I understood he knew I wasn't checking his shit, but damn, he could've deleted it. After the video, he told her text him and left his number. She left her number also and told him she would be calling from that number. After that, there was nothing else to see.

I logged out of his inbox but I made sure to screenshot the shit. I wished like hell I could get a hold of his phone because there was no telling what else I would see. Crazy part, I wasn't even mad. It actually made me feel better because I wouldn't have to feel guilty about Chaotic and me. Instead of going off on Ru, I sent the screen shots to Chaotic, and he called instantly.

"Hey."

"Who 'dat?"

"That's him. Him and some bitch talking on his inbox."

"Damn," was all Chaotic said because one thing he wouldn't do was speak down on a nigga. "So what now?"

"Shit, this all I needed to see. Now I won't feel bad about being with you. I'mma use it as my way out."

"Yeah, a'ight." He chuckled and went silent.

"I'mma call you right back."

"A'ight."

We disconnected, and I dialed Ru.

"What's up, shorty?"

"Nothing, where you at?"

"The hood 'bout to be on my way home."

"Oh, okay. Well, I was thinking 'bout that little thing we talked about. I think I wanna use Jami."

"And why is that?"

"I don't know. Maybe because I'm comfortable with her."

"Oh."

"Eventually, we gon' bring in a fourth too." I pursed my lips, ready for his reply.

"A fourth?"

"Yep. A nigga too."

"Is that right? And who is this nigga? Somebody you fucking?"

"Nah. I'll figure it out. I wanna have some fun, that's all." I giggled feeling like a pimp. "I'll hit you back, though. We'll talk about it."

"Mmm-hmm," was all he replied, and I hung up.

I swear this shit was getting crazier and crazier. Once again, the nigga didn't say no, and it tripped me out.

I dialed Chaotic's number, and when he answered, I began breaking things down to him about the foursome. The way he replied, I could hear the anger in his voice, so I got quiet.

"So this Nigga willing to let another nigga fuck you for some pussy?" Chaotic asked, and it sounded worse than I imagined. I didn't reply, so he continued. "This nigga really don't know your worth. Amor, I got tears in my fucking eyes right now just thinking 'bout this nigga willing to give yo' pussy away to fuck another bitch. This shit crazy. I'm 'bout to lie down. I'll hit you back." He hung up before I could reply.

It made me regret telling him, but he needed to know the extent Ru would go. I also wanted Chaotic to understand there was no love left. It was actually bittersweet because now, I wouldn't have to hide, but then again, Chaotic prolly thought I was foolish. Just as Chaotic, I was gonna go lie down because this shit was a bit overwhelming. Before I did, I went to the bar and took a couple shots of Hennessy to calm me down. Before I knew it, I was good and drunk, so I knew I would sleep better.

I wasn't gon' say shit to Ru about what I saw in his inbox because like I said before, I ain't give a fuck. However, the nigga ain't have to worry about me any longer. Shit was gonna slap him in the face, and when it did, he would regret losing me. Mark my words.

My eyes popped open in the wee hours of the night. Ru was

on top of me, and I could feel the moisture from the oil he used to slide inside of me with. When he saw my eyes open, he began to pound inside of me harder, and with each pound, I asked him what the fuck was he doing. This nigga had caught me while I was passed out, oiled his dick up, and had a full-blown fuck session with himself. If this wasn't some creep shit, I didn't know what was. As he continued to stroke me, the smell of alcohol seeped through his pores, and I knew then he was wasted. A few more strokes, and he bust his nut, so I jumped up from the bed and grabbed my phone.

I ran full speed into the restroom, and I was sure he thought I was going to wipe up. I sat down on the toilet, and a pool of tears began pouring from my eyes. The crazy part was, I wasn't crying because of what Ru had done. My emotions ran wild because I felt like I was cheating on Chaotic. When I looked down at my phone, I had a few missed calls and three texts from Chaotic. My heart began to race as I contemplated what I was gonna say.

Man I already knew that was coming

I mean what you think the nigga still sleeping with you every night 😡 😔

I'm bout to go to sleep I'll hit you in the am

I'm sorry 😢

I swear I never meant for that to happen

No talk to me I'm up for the night

I love you 🤍 🤍 🏁 👊 😢

Chaotic!!!

Canyon!!!!!!!!!!!!!! 😡

!

!

Delivered

iMessage

I stayed locked away in the restroom so long that my legs got numb. Right now, I didn't know how to feel because Chaotic was hurt, and I was sure Ru was wondering what I was doing. When I finally gathered myself, I headed out of the restroom and climbed into the shower. I let the hot water run over me, and

I couldn't help the tears that constantly escaped my eyes. Just thinking of hurting Chaotic did something to me, and it made me realize this shit was getting more serious by the day.

After letting the water mask my tears for about thirty minutes, I finally soaped up and stepped out. I wrapped myself in a towel and tiptoed into my bedroom, so I could slide into a pair of tights and a tee. Ru was sound asleep, and it didn't surprise me. However, that was good because he wouldn't see that I had been crying. After I was done dressing, I lay on top of the covers and as far away from Ru as possible. The way I was feeling, I knew I wasn't going to sleep anytime soon, so I basically just stared at the ceiling.

Before I knew it, the ray of the sun began peeking through the cracks of the blackout curtains I had. I knew now this was gonna be a long day, and mentally, I really wasn't prepared.

Chapter 15 Chaotic

"Hello?"

"What's up, Cedes?"

"Who 'dis?"

"Who is this?" I chuckled because the bitch knew exactly who it was. "Man, you know who the fuck it is. Anyway, I ain't calling for no bullshit. I just need you to take the rest of that bread to my moms. How much is it anyway?"

"It ain't shit."

"What you mean, 'it ain't shit.' There should've been at least forty bands left."

"You spent that, Canyon."

"Get off the phone Mercedes, and come suck this dick." I heard a nigga's voice in the background.

I knew he was only saying it because he heard her say my name, but I ain't sweat it. I didn't want the bitch no more, and it'd been like that since before I came.

"Hold up," she replied to the nigga, and I chuckled.

"So my bread just gone? Just like that?"

"What you want me to say, Canyon? I been putting that shit on yo' books and using it for bills. You know I'm not working, so what was I supposed to do?"

"Shit, let yo' nigga take care of you. You sucking his dick, and he ain't paying yo' bills?" Again, I chuckled, and she smacked her lips. "But, yeah, go suck dick. I need to call my wife."

Again, she smacked her lips, and before she could get slick, I hung up. She began calling my phone back to back, but I ignored every call. I knew the bitch had probably spent the rest of my money, but a nigga was hoping her money-hungry ass left something. I was only gonna use it to help Amor open her store front, but I ain't sweat because I had bread stashed in my mom's crib. Although I was mad at Amor at this moment, I couldn't be mad at the situation. I knew in my heart her giving that nigga my pussy was bound to happen. She still slept with the nigga every night, so in his mind, she was still his bitch.

Instead of calling Amor, I logged into my Facebook; something I hadn't done in a while. I began scrolling through her page, and the shit made me not only mad but hurt. Every picture she posted was her and the baby, and I could see in her eyes she looked broken. This wasn't Amor. Baby girl was so full of life; it pained me to see her like this. I knew it wasn't only that nigga. I was helping feed the problem by being away. One thing I knew if I ain't know shit else, and that was that girl loved the fuck outta me. I remembered those days sitting in that cell through trial, and all I asked for was God to let me go home to that girl. Although I was on my way out the gate, I still felt like I was failing her because she needed me. In a sense, I felt like I was being selfish because I wanted her to leave that nigga, but I wouldn't be there physically. On many occasions, Amor would cry about how much she was missing me. Our first visit, she cried, and I knew that came from loneliness.

After battling with my thoughts, I decided to just say fuck it and make her my wife officially. I really ain't wanna marry her behind these prison walls, but knowing that nigga was fucking up with what was mine had me ego tripping. I was down to about a year left on my time, and even though that shit would breeze by, I needed to get full custody.

After going through Amor's entire Facebook, I pulled out my notepad and began writing her a letter. With the letter, I was gonna attach some marriage papers and demand she signed them. I wasn't playing with this girl any longer; therefore, I was gonna give her my last name, and she needed to get rid of the nigga.

Normally, I wouldn't be on no shit like this, but after the screen shots she sent, that nigga ain't deserve her. Not to mention, the whole shit about the foursome. Now the threesome was something I could expect because most men were into that. The foursome he didn't deny was what had me on ten. Just hearing her tell me he agreed had me ready to break out this prison and hurt the nigga. Amor was precious to me, and it was like the nigga was taking her for granted.

I wrote her a four-page letter, and just like I said, I attached the marriage papers to them. I finally decided to call her, and I was gonna tell her I was sending them. I dialed her number and waited for her to answer. After four rings, she finally answered, and she sounded drained. I knew it was because I hadn't called or replied to the texts she sent, but she had to understand I needed to get my mind right.

"What's up?"
"Wow, so you finally decide to call me?"
"I been getting my mind right, that's all."

"But that's not fair to me, Canyon." The way she said my name, I knew she was mad.

"Shit, life ain't fair," I replied, thinking 'bout that nigga fucking her. "Check it out, though. I'm 'bout to send you these marriage papers, so sign 'em and send 'em back."

"Marriage papers?"

"You heard what the fuck I said. Get it done."

"How the fuck am I gonna do that?"

"What you mean?"

"Canyon, like let's be for real."

"So you can be my bitch, but not my wife? So basically you choosing that nigga?"

"No, I'm not choosing him. That's the problem. If you send them, I have to sign them. I can't just do that."

"Yeah, a'ight." I got quiet because I was now frustrated.

"So you're mad again?"

"Nah, I ain't mad. Shit over with."

We both got silent and just breathed into the phone. I couldn't even front; she was basically telling me no, and I knew it was because of him. The shit only added to the headache I had, so I told her I was gonna go to medical. I hung the phone up without telling her I loved her, and that was something I never did. At any given moment, anything could happen to me in here, so I made sure to always tell her I loved her. However, today, I wasn't on that type of time. I was not only mad but hurt, so I went on about my day stressed out.

❤☐☐☐

"Betterman, what's up?"

I looked up, and Ms. Rodriguez was standing in front of my cell. It was like this bitch never went home. Because anytime I needed something or to be let out, she was the one to come.

"I need to go to medical. My head been hurting for a few days," I told her.

She looked at me for a brief moment, then racked the gate. She led me down the tier and out the building to medical. When we walked into the building, she instructed me to go into a room and have a seat. Moments later, she came back and told me the nurse would be in soon. She couldn't leave me because she had to escort me back to my cell, so we both just stood here and ain't say shit. I caught her watching me from the side of her eyes, and it wasn't one of those 'watch an inmate' type of looks.

"Ms. Rodriguez, what yo' fine ass doing working in a place like this with these thirsty niggas? Where yo' husband at?"

"I don't have a husband. And I'm a big girl. These niggas don't put fear in me."

"Yeah, them niggas don't, but I do."

"Whatever, Betterman." She rolled her eyes, followed by a lip smack.

I jumped down from the bed and got into her personal space. I grabbed her chin, and she quickly moved. I grabbed her again, and this time, she just looked at me.

"Whatever, my ass. I know I make you nervous. I make every bitch nervous."

"You don't make me..." she went to say, but it was quickly cut off by a gasp because I brushed my dick against her. Because I ain't had no pussy in a while, my dick got hard, so I knew she felt the girth of it.

"Touch it," I told her, but she didn't budge. "Touch it, now," I demanded, and again, she looked at me. However, she reached out for it, so I stuck her hand inside my pants. "Now stroke it," I told her, and she began stroking as much as she could.

"How many inmates before me?"

"About five."

"So that's about an hour wait, right?"

She nodded her head *yes*.

I walked back over to the bed and jumped on top. I pulled my dick from my pants and told her to come suck it. She hesitated for a moment, but I could tell she was a freak, and this was exactly what she wanted. She walked over to the bed and stood slightly behind the curtain where she couldn't be seen. She had hesitation in her eyes, but that didn't stop her from bending down and wrapping her lips around my dick. When she got it fully wet, I wrapped my hand around the back of her neck so I didn't fuck up her sleek ponytail. I began guiding her up and down until my entire dick disappeared down her throat.

"I knew you was a real freak. Suck that muthafucka until I nut." I forcefully eased her head up and down.

She began doing something with her tongue that made my dick grow bigger. I titled my head back so I could get a clear vision of Amor. Just thinking of Amor sucking my dick made me force her to go faster. She had my shit dripping with spit as she continued to take it down her throat. When I felt myself about to nut...

"Fuck, Amor, I'm about to nut," I called out, and my legs began shaking. "Fuckkkk!" I growled as I emptied all my nut down her throat, and the bitch never stopped sucking.

She sucked my dick until every last drop had come out and my shit went soft. When she pulled back, she looked at me, and I already knew why. I slid my dick back into my pants and told her let's roll. My headache had gone away, and I was ready to get back to my cell and call my wife. I didn't know if I was feeling guilty or what, but I needed to hear her voice.

As we walked back into my unit, Ms. Rodriguez didn't say a word. She walked me into my cell and locked the gate. Before she walked off, she looked in between the bars.

"I can't believe you called me her while I was doing that." She mugged me and turned to walk away.

"That's my bitch, so deal with it," I replied and headed further into my cell.

She had me all the way fucked up if she thought she was doing something. I just needed to relieve some stress, and she was the right bitch to do it. Dismissing her bullshit, I pulled out my phone, and I had a text from Amor.

My Gutta Baby: *Chaotic, I Love You!*

Was all the text read. I read it over and over as if it would change, then fell into a daze. Granted, I was mad at her, but after what I had just done, a nigga was feeling guilty. I was feeling so guilty I didn't bother to reply. Instead, I climbed on my bed and just lay here. I got lost in my thoughts until I drifted off to sleep.

Chapter 16 Amor

After reading a four-page letter from Chaotic, I was in my feelings and in the worst mental headspace. I looked at the marriage papers he had sent, and I was stuck between a rock and hard place. I knew I had to sign them because I didn't wanna hurt him. Then, there was that part of me that didn't wanna crush Ru. Although I wasn't fucking with Ru, I just wasn't a fucked up person. I had conscious issues, and I've been like this my entire life. I was never the type to deceive someone no matter how much fucked up shit they did to me. I would let them dig their own grave and suffer after when they realized I was a stand up person.

Right now, Chaotic had my back against the wall, but he

pretty much left me no choice. I needed to talk to him first and make sure this was what he wanted. Sometimes, I still had my doubts because I was gambling with my life. I knew he loved me, but I also thought about him coming home and doing him. If I left Ru today, where I was content, I'd be made a fool if Chaotic got out and hurt me. Then I had to rethink the whole situation because I was already foolish for staying with Ru.

Instead of signing the papers, I sent Chaotic a text to call me. Within five minutes, my phone was ringing, and I answered nervously.

"What's up, ma?" he spoke coolly into the phone, and I could tell his demeanor had changed since we last spoke.

"Loving you, missing you."

"I love you and miss you too. When you coming up here?"

"Why, you finally wanna see me?"

"Hell yeah."

"I'll be there Sunday. I got your letter today."

"Shit, you already told me you ain't signing the papers, so why you saying it like that?"

"It's not that, Canyon. I just need to be sure this is what you want."

"Hell yeah, this what I want. I prayed for this, Amor."

"And I wished for it, but sometimes, I have my doubts. Like, you have to understand that I'm gambling with my life. Despite the circumstances, I've proved to you I'm down with you. Canyon, you haven't gotten a chance to prove shit."

"So now I gotta prove myself? That's crazy because you act like this your relationship. Amor, I'm the one who wanted this from the gate. I didn't come into yo' life to play games with you and taint yo' heart. A nigga really loves you. You act like I got life. I only got a year left. I could have a million bitches running to this muthafucka. I could've had a million bitches running to court, but I kept a clean slate. If you need time because you think I'mma hurt you, then I'll marry you when I get out so I can prove myself."

"It's not like that." I sighed with frustration.

That sarcastic ass *prove myself* told me he wasn't getting

what the fuck I was saying. I was willing to become this man's wife. This was something I had imagined for an eternity. I just wanted to be sure. I knew he probably thought it was because of Ru, but Ru wasn't the case. I mean, he played a part in it, but that wasn't just it.

"Aye, how much you need for your store?" he changed the subject.

"I don't know. I have to just lease a building and purchase everything to decorate it. Not to mention, I have to buy bulks of clothing."

"Can you do all that with thirty bands?"

"Yeah, but why you asking me that?"

"Because I'mma give you the money, ma."

"No, I'm fine, babe. Just wait until you get out, and we'll talk about it," I stressed because I didn't want him spending any money, and he still had time to do.

He needed it more than me. I smiled hard just hearing him say he was gonna help me open my boutique.

"I'm not waiting for shit. I know this is what you want, so I'mma give you everything you desire. I wanted to give you more, but I talked to ol' girl, and the bitch spent the money I had left on the streets." He continued to ramble, and everything he was saying pretty much flew past my head because all I could focus on was him calling his ex.

"So you called the bitch?" I stopped him dead in his tracks.

"Yeah. I called her for my money."

"Whatever, nigga. Let me find out you still been talking to that bitch."

"Hell nah. I just told you why I called. Stop tripping. Don't nobody want yo' nigga."

"That's the problem. *Everybody* wants my nigga. Boy, we can't even have a good visit without these thirsty hoes eye-fucking you. Even the police bitches be admiring you right in my face."

"But I don't see nobody but you. I don't give a fuck how many bitches in one room. Amor, you the only chick I want and love. It's been that way. Amor, you think a nigga really playing with you, huh?"

"No," I replied, wondering why he said it like that.

As we continued to talk, I began scrolling through Facebook. Canyon's page popped up, and I stopped because a picture of me was posted from his page. The caption read...

I'm stuck to these streets, I'm sprung on this loot
Addicted to crime, but I'm attracted to you #BF

Which was a Nipsey Hussle lyric and attached was a picture of me.

"Canyon!" I called out to him, shocked he had posted it. "When did you post this pic?"

"Why, it's a problem?"

"No. Ummm..." I lied because I was really shitting bricks.

I knew Ru would see it or definitely someone would tell him. Not only did he have Mercedes as a friend, but he and Chaotic had thirty-six more mutual friends.

"Amor, I don't give a fuck about shit. You my bitch, and I keep telling you that. I'm tired of playing with you. I'm tired of playing with you. You lucky I put that *BF* shit!" he barked, and I couldn't do shit but stare into the air. This man was really crazy, and now shit was gonna hit the fan.

Moving around the house, I had just finished cleaning and was now chopping bell peppers and onions for my dinner. Ru had gone to the city to make a large quantity of weed sale, so it was just Heaven and I. It was only 5:40 in the evening, and she was knocked out asleep because of the bath I had given her. While I was back and forth from the stove, I was sitting at the dinner table browsing online for a building. Before Chaotic and I hung up, he instructed me to pick some money up from his mom to open the boutique. No matter how many times I told him no, he wouldn't take no for an answer.

The sound of my phone began ringing, and I knew it was Chaotic, so I quickly ran to the table to answer. When I looked at the screen, it was Ru, so I quickly answered because he was prolly in the store grabbing me a couple cans of cream of chicken.

"Hey, you there?"

"Bitch, on my mama, I'm fucking you up!" he shouted into the phone furiously.

"What are you talking about?"

"You know what the fuck I'm talking about. *Fuck you!*" He hung up the phone, and a message came through.

It was the screenshot from Chaotic's page, and a screenshot of a few comments. I leaned on the sink and just looked at the screenshots. I contemplated what I would say when he got home until I realized that nigga wasn't no damn saint either. I continued to cook my meal and prepared myself for the rapture.

When Ru flew through the door, I knew he had to be flying on the freeway because he was home in no time. All I saw was the back of his head as he stormed into the bedroom. The sound of rambling and doors slamming told me he was in the room packing his shit. Normally, I would be on some *Baby Boy* shit blocking the doorway, but because my heart wasn't there any longer, I let him pack.

When I walked into the room, all of his clothing was laid on the floor and some were in bags. I took a seat on the bed, and neither of us said a word. Once he was done packing, he came back into the room and just looked at me. I didn't look him in the eyes, but I could feel him burning a hole through the side of my face. He then walked over and took a seat at my vanity. He dropped his head, then the questions began.

"So you fuck with that nigga, huh?"

"Nah."

"That nigga wouldn't just be posting you. Man, I knew this shit. All along, y'all been sneaking and creeping behind my back."

"I just told you I don't fuck with him."

"Well, delete him."

"No, I'm not deleting him." I looked at him as if he were crazy.

"Either you delete the nigga, or I'm leaving." He stood to his feet.

"I'm not deleting him, Ru." I stood my ground.

If I deleted Canyon, then I would hurt him because that would look like I chose Ru. I looked at Ru and couldn't believe he had based this whole relationship on deleting a nigga from social media. Fuck my feelings. Fuck the reason we came to this. Fuck my tears, and most importantly, fuck the family we had built. All because of his image on social media. He looked at me hard, as if he couldn't believe I denied deleting Chaotic, and a tear slid down his face. He walked over to the mirror but remained quiet as he stared at his own reflection.

"Yeah, you fuck with that bitch ass nigga," he spoke, watching me through the mirror.

I gave him the same look he was giving me because he really had his fucking nerves when he was cheating with a bitch he met on Facebook.

"You and I both know he ain't no bitch," I mumbled but loud enough for him to hear me.

Before I knew it, he ran over to me and wrapped his hands around my neck. I fell back onto the bed, gasping for air as he continued to squeeze the life out of me. Ru was choking me hard as he cried a pool of tears. This nigga was trying to kill me, and all I could think about was the gun in my closet. Suddenly, he snapped back to reality because he finally let me go. Tears now fell from my eyes because never in my wildest years would I expect Ru to put his hands on me. My throat was hurting as if he had busted a vessel, but I wasn't crying from the pain. Never would I have thought Ru would put his hands on me. This was some shit we both couldn't come back from, and whether we both were content in this relationship, it was time we both went our separate ways.

"I get caught up one time, and you go into a rage. All the times I caught you cheating, and you got the nerves to act like this. You got a whole bitch you met on Facebook who's sending you pussy videos, and you got the muthafucking nerve to be crying."

He looked at me shocked because he didn't know I knew. I could see the guilt all over his face, but that wasn't gonna change shit.

"Yeah, yo' little bitch, Tina, can have you. So get the fuck on, nigga!" I stormed off and headed into my daughter's room.

I took a seat on her bed and watched as Ru walked back and forth from the room to his car filling it up with his belongings. As I sat here, all the great times Ru and me had flashed through my mind, but the bad outweighed the good, so I knew I wouldn't miss shit. I lay down next to my daughter still in disbelief that he had put his hands on me.

I could hear my phone ringing from the kitchen, but I was so consumed with my thoughts I didn't bother answering it. I lay next to my baby as tears continued to pour from my eyes, and when I heard the door slam, I knew he was gone. The misery was finally over, and the Lord was preparing me for a new journey. None of this had come about because of a nigga; I let Ru walk away for my own happiness, and already, I felt a sense of peace.

Chapter 17 Chaotic

Two Weeks Later

To: My Husband (Big Poppa)
From: Your Wife (Gutta Baby)
Date: September 21st, 2019
Time: 3:18am
Dedication: Beyonce "Dangerously In Love"

Dear Chaotic,

As I write this letter I have a tribe of butterflies flying through my stomach. The shit so krazy because as comfortable as I am with you now I still get nervous. I can't help it. I guess it's because I've never been in love like this. Loving you is like a fairytale, so it feels unbelievable. Canyon I've never loved like this! And truthfully I don't think I'll ever love like this again. I swear I love tf outta you. Everything about you! From the way you eat chicken to the way you walk (yes I be watching you walk to the restroom while visiting) lol. I can give you way more than 25 reasons why I'm in love with you but I'm not gone go there. However, I will say, most of all I love the way you love me. Every time you tell me "ain't nobody gonna love you like me" you say that shit with not only meaning but so fkn sincere. You've shown me in so many ways that's a true statement and you ain't lying because nobody has loved me like you. Not my family, a nigga ...NOBODY!!!

And just for that reason, you deserve every ounce of love I have to give. I would never imagine in a million years that Ru and I would be over with but for you I'd go to war with God. I know people were affected by our breakup but for the first time I chose myself over the world. All I ever wanted was a man to love me for me and make me happy; which was never too much to ask. I've always thought that "love doesn't exist in my world" but you came along and changed my frame of mind. In the past I had been hurt, taken for granted and misunderstood so much I gave up on the entire ideal of love. Then this happened. Boy yo sexy ass came in, ski masked down, laid the whole house down and stole my mf heart. Soon I'll be Mrs. Betterman and give you a beautiful baby you keep asking for. I'm going to end this letter with...I'll never have any regrets by the decisions I made in my life. With you I feel secure and I know my heart won't let me down. I love you fiancé and we will be as one soon.

Ps...I can't wait until we make love under the moon and next time I'm in control. Love, Your Wife 4 Life.

After reading Amor's letter for about the tenth time, I waited for my name to be called for our visit. Although our visits were frequent, and we talked on the phone, I wanted so badly to reply to her letter. The shit touched every emotion I had, and I would fasho bring it up at our visit. However, I was still gonna reply because when it came to those letters, a nigga could get deep. It was always hard for me to express myself in person, but with Amor, I tried.

I stood to my feet when I heard my name, and just like the first visit, my heart was pounding. Not only because of this touching ass letter, but this was our first visit with me having full custody. Amor officially belonged to me, and ol' boy was now out of the picture.

I headed down the hall, out the building, and into visiting. When I made it, I did the normal routine by handing in my ID, then I was instructed to table forty-two. I smiled when the CO told me the table number because this table was in the far back, and they couldn't watch my every move. In here, these CO's stayed on my ass because they knew what I was doing. Not only that, but I pretty much ran the yard. I had the niggas who were somebody to these other niggas making me rice bowls and running my packs.

"Babyyy." I smiled wide at Amor as she stood to her feet. I pulled her into my embrace and kissed her long and forcefully. "I love you, ma." I pulled back before the CO said something, and we took our seat.

"I love you too, babe." She blushed.

"Why yo' ass so shy?" I chuckled because no matter how tough she was or how long we fucked around, I still made this girl nervous.

"I don't know," she squealed like a little ass girl and shrugged her shoulders.

I pulled her hands into mine and looked her in the eyes. I was trying hard to read her, and the look in her eyes was assuring. Granted, she told me she didn't regret the decision she made, but it was easier said than done. Looking in her eyes was justification, and I now believed her.

"Where the baby? I thought you was bringing her."

"She's with Ru."

"They at the house?"

"They at his mom's house," she replied, and I could tell she was nervous, but I wasn't tripping. One thing I wasn't was threatened by no nigga. I understood they had a child together, and he would still be around. "Just because he comes over doesn't mean he's coming back. All his shit still gone. He just comes to see Heaven. We don't say much to each other. He goes to Heaven's room, and that's where he spends his time."

"I'm not tripping off that nigga, ma. I know he bet not be

tryna fuck you, though."

"Hell nah, that's out. That chapter of my life is over with, and I'm happy now."

"Aww, I make you happy, baby girl?"

"Yes. I know it sounds crazy because you would expect me to have some sort of feelings about the situation considering the years we'd been together, but, no. On my daughter, I ain't missed the nigga once."

I nodded my head because that was something I really couldn't speak on. It was good to know she wasn't having doubts, but still, I couldn't speak on it.

"Let's get something to eat, ma."

I stood up and pulled her hand so she could stand. We went to the vending machines, and just like always, we ordered rotisserie chicken, rice, and a couple bags of chips. We then headed over to the microwave, and while I began warming the rice, Amor headed back to the vending machine to grab our sodas. I turned around just in time to see her bend down to get the sodas out the machine, and instantly, I got mad. I ran over to her...

"What the fuck you doing?" I slightly pushed her so she could stand up. I bent down into the machine to get the soda, then looked at her like she was crazy.

"I was getting our sodas."

"Man, yo' ass bending over and shit. The fuck wrong with you?"

"I have on this long ass dress, Canyon." She frowned, shocked that I was tripping.

"What type of niggas you be fucking with be letting you bend over and shit?" I shook my head and headed to the microwave with her behind me.

After getting the rice, we headed outside to our table and took our seats. We began eating our food, but I could barely eat because I was still fuming.

"Wow, so you really tripping over me bending down to get yo' fucking soda?"

"Nah," I replied and grabbed a napkin.

"Yes, you are. Damn, I'm sorry, and it won't happen again." She dropped her head and picked at the meat.

"Damn right it ain't gon' happen again. Look, I don't give a fuck. We can be in the market, and I'm on aisle twenty-five and you on two. If you need canned goods, you call me, and I'm coming. I don't give a fuck if you need yo' shoes tied. You call me, and I'm coming. A woman ain't supposed to be bending over and shit."

"Okay," she replied and wrapped her arm into mine. "Stop tripping, please." She gave me her little puppy eyes, and of course, it worked.

I reached over and kissed her on the cheek, then continued to eat my food. We began chatting, and after a while, I wasn't tripping, so we were laughing again.

When we were done eating, I took the trash inside and brought out the Connect Four that she said she wanted to play. Instead of sitting across from her, I sat next to her. Inmates weren't supposed to sit next to visitors, but I didn't give a fuck. One thing I did was break rules and didn't give a fuck who set them.

"I'm 'bout to kick yo' ass." She laughed, rubbing her hands together.

"Girl, I play chess. This shit easy." I grabbed the blue chips and began stacking them in front of me. We began to play as we talked, and the sudden brushing of Amor's leg on mine made my dick grow. "Feel this." I grabbed her hand under the table and put it on my dick.

"Damn," she spoke in a low tone, and I could tell she was turned on.

Without me telling her to, she looked around, and when the cost was clear, she stuck her hand into my pants. She began stroking my dick while I looked around to make sure no one saw us. My dick was so hard all I had was my imagination, and thoughts of the sexy lingerie pictures she had sent me popped in my head. I slid my hand under the table, on the low, and pulled her dress up just enough for me to have access to her pussy. I used two fingers to slide her panties to the side, then inserted those same fingers in her. I began toying around in her pussy, and I could hear light moans escaping her lips. I had her so gone she lost focus of stroking my dick and grabbed the umbrella on the table.

"Ma, yo' ass 'bout to get us cracked," I whispered into her ear because she had zoned out on me.

She opened her eyes and looked around remembering we were sitting in this visiting room.

"Damn, yo' pussy wet as fuck."

I frowned because I wanted to dive into her bad as a muthafucka. I stuck my fingers into her as far as I could and started going harder. When I felt her leg trembling and the hot liquid spilling onto my fingers, I knew she had nutted. I pulled my fingers from inside of her, and they were covered in white juices. I took them both into my mouth and sucked every drop off, then looked at her.

"I'mma fuck the shit outta you when I come home. I spared you the last time, but this time, I'mma kill that shit," I told her, then looked up.

I locked eyes with Ms. Rodriguez, and the shit made me freeze. She was looking dead at us, and the only thing I could do was smirk. I sucked on my fingers again to let her know Amor's juices tasted sweet like candy. She mugged me, then turned to walk away. Right then, I knew that bitch was gonna be a problem.

Chapter 18 Amor

When I made it to my car after my visit, I was smiling from ear to ear. Despite me getting dumped for about an hour for bending over, I had the best visit on earth. I climbed into the driver seat and pulled my phone from the glove box. I noticed I had several missed calls from Ru. I quickly called him because Chaotic was about to call, so I wanted to get Ru out the way.

Ever since the day he left, guilt from him putting his hands on me was eating at him. I didn't let him come back, but he did come a few times to see Heaven. Most of the time, I was in my bedroom, on the phone with Chaotic, and I knew Ru knew exactly who I was talking to. Chaotic had begun to post me more, and I was sure that had gotten back to Ru if he hadn't seen the shit for himself.

"What's up, man? I been calling you," Ru spoke into the phone with urgency.

"I was busy, what's up?"

"Man, I was locked up. I just had to bail out." He got quiet as if I was supposed to show sympathy.

"Okay, and what you telling me for? Where's my daughter?"

"Wow. Yeah, a'ight. She's straight, but I'll let you go." He disconnected the phone, and I didn't bother calling back.

One thing I knew about Ru was, he always used empathy to try and get me. The other day when he walked in, he told me about his grandmother being sick. I wasn't trying to be a bitch, but I knew what he was doing, so I didn't give him the reaction he was looking for.

I pulled out of the parking lot and cruised down a small highway that led to the freeway home. Just as I got onto the freeway, Chaotic was calling, and those same damn butterflies began emerging.

"You miss me already?" I answered with a huge grin.

"Hell yeah," he replied, and I could hear his smile through the phone. "You enjoyed yo' visit?"

"Hell yeah. Other than yo' ass dumping me, I had fun."

He chuckled. "Man, I ain't dump yo' ass. You just need to learn me and the shit I don't go for. We good, tho', baby."

"On my way out, that CO bitch who was in visiting was mugging me hard."

"Is that right? Which one?"

"The Hispanic one, kinda thick."

"I think I know who you talkin 'bout. Yeah, she prolly just on us because what we were doing in visiting. You know we can lose our visits for that?"

"Yeah, I know, but fuck them people."

Again, he chuckled and replied. "You right. So you on your

way home, or you going to get the baby?"

"I'mma go get my baby."

"A'ight, then. Get yo' ass back on that freeway."

"I am, baby, with yo' crazy ass. I swear you remind me so much of The Joker."

"You always say that."

We shared a laugh as I merged into another lane.

"It's true. You just be smiling while you terrorize the world. Not only that, but I just tripped off how at one point, you were scared to love me, but nothing in the world put fear in you. Now it seems like I'm all you care about."

"Amor, you my favorite person in the world." He spoke with so much sincerity.

Damn. I paused because he had knocked the wind out of me. I didn't expect him to say no shit like that, and it was passionate. "Man, you just know all the right shit to say, huh?" I smirked. "I love you, Chaotic."

"I love you too, Gutta Baby."

❤️□□□

I pulled up to Ru's mother's home, and when I didn't see his car, I pulled along the curb and dialed his number.

"Yeah?" he answered as if he didn't wanna be bothered.

"Where are you? I'm here to get the baby."

"I ran around the corner. I'm 'bout to pull back up."

"A'ight."

I hung up and turned my engine off. I began scrolling through my phone and texting back and forth with Chaotic.

I watched as Ru's car pulled into the driveway, and he climbed out. He ran into the house, and minutes later, he came out holding Heaven and her diaper bag. He put her into her car seat, then buckled her inside. After kissing her on the cheek, he closed the door and went to the passenger side of my car. He looked at me, and I could tell he wanted to talk. However, there wasn't much to say, so he brought up his new case.

"Yeah, a nigga bout to be fighting a case," he spoke, and instead of asking him why the fuck he was telling me, I let him vent. "Because of my record, I might have to do a couple years."

"Damn," I replied. What else was I supposed to say?

"Damn, you all at visits and shit?"

I looked over, and Ru was reading the visiting slip that set on the seat. He shook his head and walked away from the car. Again, what the fuck was I supposed to say? I pulled off before the nigga came back and added some slick shit that would make me curse his ass out.

By the time I made it to the highway, I got a text, and it was from Ru.

Ruger >

That's brazy asf you really fuck with blood. Not only is he a enemy but the nigga was just locked up for yo little bro murder. So what he ain't do it his homies did and you fucking with the nigga. What's really brazy is you ain't give us a chance. When two ppl married they work shit out but you just throw everything away SMH

That's the thing Ru, we wasn't married. Remember I wasn't good enough for you to marry

Delivered

  iMessage

After reading the texting and keeping shit short and simple, I dropped my phone into the cup holder because I ain't have shit else to say. I couldn't believe the nigga brought up my brother, but I didn't sweat it. I knew he was only trying to make me feel guilty and make Chaotic look bad. I really couldn't believe the nigga had the audacity to mention marriage as if we had tied the knot. All of a sudden, we were married.

After that nigga proposed to me, marriage was never brought up again. I mean, I mentioned it once or twice, and when he brushed me off, I left the shit alone. As time went by and our love faded, I didn't wanna be married because I didn't wanna get married to a cheater. Ru had left the doors open for Chaotic, so the ideal of marriage was far from my mind. I had begun falling for Chaotic, and when I realized my heart craved that man, he was the only one fit to become my husband.

I really ain't see a future with Ru; we just stayed together and lived for the moment. With Chaotic, shit was different. He loved me, secured me, and saw a bright future for me. The way he indulged in my business and insisted on buying my boutique let me know he believed in me and only wanted to see me happy. Ru, on the other hand, half-listened when I talked about my business, and my boutique was what paid the bills.

Just like I told Chaotic, that chapter in my life was over, and I was finally smiling. I felt alive for the first time in years and just the thought alone hurt me. I totally let myself go and put my own happiness aside to make sure Ru was happy; but he wasn't. Which was why I didn't understand how could he act so broken. That man didn't love me, and the statement was true when they said you don't miss what you have until it was gone. His lost.

Chapter 19 Amor

I moved around Jami's home a nervous wreck. I just got done getting dressed, and she curled my hair for me. Today was the day I was gonna meet Chaotic's mother to get the money for the boutique. I talked to her on the phone a few times, and she was hella cool, but this was our first time meeting in person.

Once I was done, I went into the living room to kiss Heaven, who was in front of the TV watching *Mickey Mouse Clubhouse*. She barely paid me attention, but she waved her little hand *bye* without looking at me.

"Okay, Jami, I'll see you in a minute."

"Okay, boo. Have fun, and drive safe."

I walked out the door, jumped into my car, and headed for the city of Carson.

That's on my mama, yeah, that's on the hood
Don't want no problems, I wish a bitch would
Try to come between us, it won't end up good
You know I love you like no one else could

I listened to Summer Walker's *Over It* album all the way to my destination. By the time I made it, it had begun to sprinkle. I looked for the correct address, and when I saw the café, I parked and climbed out. I headed inside, and because she was the only woman sitting alone, I figured it was her.

"Moms?" I called out to her because this was what I called her.

"Hey, baby." She stood up and hugged me.

Her small frame was stacked like one of these young girls who paid for their bodies. She was brown-skinned with a short, spikey cut, and she looked exactly like Canyon.

I took a seat, and she slid me a menu.

"Their glazed waffles and chicken is good."

"I'mma try it with a side of potatoes."

"I want grits."

We waited for the waiter to come over and take our orders. We began to chat, and she began reminiscing on the past. She brought up Canyon's father from my hood. She also knew my mother, and this made me excited. By the time we were done eating, we had laughed, got very acquainted, and she told me so many stories about Chaotic. She told me things about his childhood, and I smiled through the whole conversation. Two things really stood out, and that was his love for animals, especially fish, and he played the drums. She also told me about the schools he went to, which were really great schools that you had to get accepted into. Canyon was really a great child. Somewhere along the line, he got caught up into the streets, and he was now knee deep in it.

We headed outside, and she went to the trunk of her car. She pulled out a small black bag and handed it to me.

"You found your building?"

"Yes, it's nice. I'm going when I leave here."

"I wanna see it."

"You do? Okay, follow me."

I smiled, and we both climbed into our cars. It was still lightly raining, so we drove at normal speed. My phone began to ring, and it was Chaotic, so I quickly answered.

"'Sup, Cute Face?"

"Hey, baby."

"I love you."

"I love you tooo. Thank you so much, babe."

"You ain't gotta thank me. Ma, this what I'm supposed to do. I'll do anything for you."

"Awww. I love you, man."

"I love you too. So I take it you met with Mama?"

"Yep, she behind me."

"Behind you? What you mean, 'behind you'?"

"She's following me. She wanted to see the location."

"Damn," he replied and paused. "That's crazy. My mom don't like nobody. When I say *nobody*, I mean, *nobody*."

"Well, we hit it off well. She's so cool."

"Yeah, that's because y'all both bloods." He chuckled sarcastically.

"Yeah, we exchanged hood notes. She told me about your dad too." I smiled, wishing I had met him. I was too young when my big homie was murdered, therefore, I never got to meet him. "We going to the hood after."

"Y'all, what?" he asked, and he wasn't laughing.

"I'm just playing, babe." I giggled because I knew I pissed him off.

Chaotic didn't want me in the hood since I had gotten shot. He said he didn't mind me going over there, but I needed to wait until he came home. All he wanted was to protect me, and I understood where he was coming from, so I didn't go.

"Stop playing with me, Amor."

"I was just playing."

"Where y'all at?" He changed the subject.

"'Bout to pull up in about ten minutes. I'm excited."

"Aww, you excited, ma?"

"Yes. I have so many plans for this place."

"I can't wait to see it."

A text came through my phone that I couldn't read because I was driving, but I was able to read the beginning of it. I frowned and quickly looked up to the road.

As I drove, I was texting furiously. I knew exactly who it was because I remembered the number from Ru's inbox. I wanted to call so bad because this bitch had her nerve, but for what? I really didn't give a fuck, and if I did, I would have been called. I actually stopped texting the bitch and left her at *read*. Ru brought the bitch up regularly trying hard to convince me that he never even saw her in person. Now here it was, she was texting me, and that told me it was more. Not to mention, he had to be in the bitch's presence. Because how the fuck she get my number?

We pulled up to the location and parked in the small parking lot next door. Chaotic stayed on the phone to talk to his mom, so when we met up, I handed her the phone. As they talked, we headed toward the entrance, and the owner met us at the door. He led us inside, and already, I was in love. The place was huge, and I could visualize the way I would decorate. I couldn't wait to open my boutique, and thanks to Chaotic, he made it happen.

Chaotic

"Aye, Ms. Rodriguez, I need to go to medical."

"What's wrong now?"

"My tooth hurts."

She looked at me because she knew I was lying, but that didn't stop her from opening the cell. Her eyes lit up like saucers, and I knew it was because she anticipated sucking my dick. She walked me down the tier for medical, and from time to time, she looked back and smirked. When we made it to the building, she escorted me in and instructed me to sign my name. Once I signed the paper, I was given a room to go into and have a seat.

We both walked into the room, and as she was supposed to, she stood by the door with her hand on her belt the way she was trained. She looked out the door continuously, then at me. Instead of sitting on the bed as I was supposed to, I stood slightly behind the curtain.

"Come here," I told her.

She hesitated but came. When she got into my reach, I looked her in the eyes, and I could see the freakiness in her. I raised my hand and wrapped it around her neck. She looked at me with her eyes bulging because I began applying pressure. She began gagging and gasping for air, and I looked at her disgustingly.

"If you ever in yo' muthafucking life look in my wife's direction, I'll kill you with my bare fucking hands. You got that?" I asked her as my eyes went black.

She began nodding her head as she continued choking. "Pleeeee...plea..." She tried to speak, and I finally let her go. She bent down trying hard to catch her breath, and when she did, she looked at me crazy.

I didn't give a fuck about that because what could she really do? Bitch couldn't tell because she was already at risk of losing her job by sucking my dick. However, she did put her hand on her gun, and that shit didn't scare me. I laughed in the bitch's face and walked away from her, right out medical. I escorted my fucking self to my building, and in the far, I could see her behind me. Because I didn't wanna get her weird ass in trouble, I stopped at the door so it could look like she was walking me in.

When she walked past me, she rolled her eyes, and again, I laughed. She led me through the door and to my cell. She unlocked it, and slammed it with so much force. I went to my bed and pulled out my phone. I didn't give a fuck if she saw me. She was still standing by my cell, but I ignored her. When she finally walked off, she mumbled some shit I didn't catch.

Any other bitch, I wouldn't have tripped like this, but this was Amor. When it came to her, I would kill anybody with no remorse. I knew it sounded crazy, but the love I had for that girl ran so deep anybody or anything that harmed her would be wrapped in a white sheet. I didn't play when it came to her, and if it meant my own life, then so be it.

While I continued to text my wife, I laughed because her ass didn't have a comeback. She thought it was funny, but I was serious. Fucking with a nigga like me, I would be scared too. It wasn't on no street shit because that was already proven; it was because I knew I could love her like she never been loved.

She saw me dropping roses for the next bitch, and that wasn't shit. I was gonna pamper Amor, and shit like roses would get dropped in her bath every night. I was the type of nigga who ran bath water. Like I said before, I'd never been in love, but I've tried my hand with a few bitches. The little bit of time we were together, I showed them how a real gangsta could be charming. This girl didn't know what I had in store for her. Everything in my plans for her was everything she deserved. Ain't no bitch ever been this loyal to me, and not to mention, she threw away her family for my love. I was gonna give her the same love, loyalty, and respect when I made it home, and that was on my granny, Queen.

For years, Amor had been living in darkness. She really ain't know her worth, and her worth was priceless. I looked at her like a Queen, and in my eyes, wasn't no bitch fading her.

"Aye, Chaotic, the nigga in his cell."

I looked up, and Rolo was at my cell. I knew exactly who he was talking about, so I jumped up from my bed and grabbed the knife I had made. Rolo began yelling down the tier for a CO to rack the gates, and within seconds, Officer Ambros was letting me out. We had five minutes to chow, so definitely, I would have an excuse to be out.

I walked the tier and took the stairs down to the first floor. There were a few inmates lingering around, but I paid them no mind. Niggas were playing chess, some were on the phones, and a few had gotten their meals early because they were trusties.

"Ayo, Frank, let me holla at you."

"Chaotic, man, I'mma have yo' bread in the morning," he began pleading.

"Let me holla at you," again, I told him, but he didn't move.

I walked over to the table where he was sitting, and the look in his eyes let me know he expected what was about to happen. I walked up on Frank, and he dropped his head. Quickly, I began sticking my knife in and out his back until his body fell onto the table. Everyone stood around because this shit was normal. I quickly moved away because the sound of the alarm had begun ringing. Because Rolo and a few niggas were surrounding me, the police had no idea what had just happened.

Everyone began to scatter for their cells, and I was ecstatic I made it away. I headed into my cell, but before I went in, Rolo took the knife to discard it. Because he was a trustee, it would be easy to get rid of the weapon. I headed over to my crock pot, powered it on, then began pulling out the items for a burrito. Like nothing ever happened, I kicked my feet up and was satisfied with the message I sent. Just like on the streets, I didn't play with my money. You play with pussy, you get fucked. That simple.

Chapter 20 Amor

S itting on my bed, I was holding Heaven as she closed her eyes, going in and out of sleep. The sound of footsteps in my home told me someone had entered, and of course, it was Ru. He still had a key that I had yet to take and used it to his advantage.

When he walked in, he looked at me, then to Heaven. He walked over to kiss her on the cheek, then pulled her into his arms. He put her on his chest, and in an instant, she finally dozed off. I sat here quietly as he took her into her bedroom and lay her down. When he walked back in, he looked at me again, but I didn't say a word. I didn't mention the bitch texting me because then it would

BARBIE SCOTT

look like I cared. He walked into the restroom, then came back within minutes. He leaned back on the dresser and just stared at me.

"Let's get married," he spoke, making me look up from my computer that I had finally grabbed.

"What?" I looked at him as if he were crazy as hell.

"Let's get married. Let's move away and start over, shorty. Another state, another country. Just far away where nobody knows us. Let's have another baby and just live." He bit his lip with a hint of nervousness.

For the first time in years, he looked so sincere. I saw pain in his eyes, and the way he stared at me told me his heart was crying out for me. I really ain't know what to say because this shit took me by surprise. He spoke words I had dreamed about for years, but this was another life. Things had changed, hearts had been broken, and love had gotten lost along with chivalry and fidelity.

"I can't, Ru." I looked him in his eyes because I needed him to understand.

"And why is that?"

"Because I owe him a chance." I dropped my head, not because I was ashamed, but because I never imagined I'd be this straight forward with Ruger.

"Damn," he replied, and I could see the tears build up in his eyes.

In another life, I prolly would have felt sorry for him, but I didn't. Why did it take for me to leave him and let another man love me, for him to wanna move away and finally make me a wife?

The sound of my phone ringing made Ru and me both look down at the bed. When I saw it was Chaotic, I let out a soft sigh because I couldn't ignore his call.

"Hey."

"I love you, ma," was the first thing he said nearly every time he called.

I looked up at Ru, and before I could reply, he walked out assuming it was Chaotic. "I love you too. I swear I do." I smiled

128

gracefully.

"I was just calling to tell you I love you. They about to do this count, so I'mma put the phone up until they done."

"Okay."

"A'ight." He hung up.

I sat here still caught up over the fact that I was head over heels in love with that man.

"That nigga really makes you happy. You should see the smile on yo' face when he calls." Ru appeared in the doorway. He shook his head and walked back out the room.

I got up from my bed to see if he was leaving, but the nigga had taken his shoes off and climbed into the bed with Heaven. I didn't say anything else. Instead, I went into my room and went to my Instagram. I typed in the name @a1_the_artist and DM'd him. When he told me he had an appointment in about three hours, I told him I could come now, and he agreed. A1 was the hottest tattoo artist in the surrounding city that I had heard of. I slid on my shoes and left the house.

❤️🖤🖤🖤

The Next Morning

When I think about how much I'm loving you
No limitations, no set of regimented rules
I'm amazed how much this love has touched my life
And the commitment that we share is a welcome sacrifice

I moved around my kitchen singing my heart out to Anita's "Just Because" as I prepared breakfast. I was whipping up some fried chicken, scrambled eggs, and steamed rice. I remembered growing up, my mother would make this for me, and I loved it.

Especially sugar in my rice, then I would mix it with the eggs. Now that Heaven was eating regular food, I noticed she loved rice and fried chicken. She hated vegetables except corn. Any kind of corn she would tear up.

Waaam!

"Awww!" I grabbed my backside and spun around.

"Aww. What the fuck you got?" Ru reached out and lifted my dress. I tried to move out of his reach because he was invading my privacy. However, it was too late; he had already seen it.

"Damn, you got the nigga name tatted?" He shook his head disappointingly.

I looked at him and didn't say a word. It really wasn't his business, so I didn't feel the need to explain shit. Last night, I got a tattoo of the Harley Quinn Rotten tattoo. It had *Big Chaotic* over the bat. It was colored in and detailed really cute. It was on my ass, so it stood out.

Ru was still standing there, but he didn't speak. He began scrolling through his phone, and I could see the same hurt in his eyes from last night. Keep shit real, I totally forgot he had stayed until I walked into Heaven's room this morning. I could only imagine what he was thinking because I was up late on the phone with Chaotic. I couldn't understand for the life of me why he came around to only hurt himself. I wasn't leaving Chaotic, and there was nothing Ru could do to make me leave.

I began making our plates and went to get Heaven so she could eat. Ru walked in and only looked at his plate. He did bother grabbing it. He went over to the table and kissed Heaven.

"Daddy be back to see you, baby," he told her, then kissed her again. He walked out without saying a word to me, and when I heard the front door close, I felt relieved.

Chapter 21 Amor

The sound of my phone ringing woke me up from a deep sleep. I was doped up from the medicine I had taken last night to sleep. Out of nowhere, I had gotten sick, and out of all the colds I ever had, this one was the worst.

"Hey, Mommy."

"Oh my God, you sound horrible."

"I got a cold."

"Have you taken anything?"

"Yes. Everything from NyQuil to Theraflu. Nothing is working. Ma, this the worst cold I ever had in my life." A tear slid down my cheek. My entire body was in pain, my breathing was off, and I had a horrible cough.

"Aww. You need me to send you a humidifier?" my mother asked with concern.

"I have one for Heaven."

"Okay, well, put some Vicks in it and get under the covers. You get some rest. I'll call you later."

"Okay. I love you."

"Love you too."

Just as I closed my eyes, a call from Chaotic came through.

"Hey, babe."

"Damn, ma, you sound fucked up." Just as my mom, he sounded concerned.

"I'm fucked up. My entire body hurts."

"Damn," was all he said, and I could tell it was bothering him. "Man, bring me your cold."

"Huh?"

"Come up here. Bring me your cold. You got that baby and shit to do. You can't afford to stay sick."

"Aww, baby." I cooed, on the verge of crying. That was so sweet, but I couldn't do it. "Babe, I can't get you sick. This cold is the worst."

"Man, what the fuck I say?" He got serious. With him, wasn't no arguing. When he spoke, that's what it was.

"Okay, Canyon. If I have the willpower to get out of bed, I'll come tomorrow."

"Please, babe. You too fucked up. You got anything you need done?"

"Like what?"

"Anything. Medicine, your boutique, anything, ma."

"I have every kind of medicine sold in stores. The boutique furniture is being delivered Monday."

"Okay, well, I can send moms up there to wait for it."

"No, it's okay. The owner of the building is doing some work for me, so he'll be there."

"A'ight. I love you, ma."

"I love you too." I smiled faintly.

No matter what, this man told me he loved me daily. I love the fuck outta him just because the way he loved me.

❤️□□□

Sitting in the visiting room waiting on Canyon, I was so sick I had my head lying on the table we were assigned. Looking around the room, I noticed a few of the women had colds. I was more than sure it was because of the weather that had been on and off with rain.

"Babyyyy."

I heard my baby's voice, so I lifted my head up, then stood to my feet.

Like always, he wrapped me in his arms, then kissed me long and hard. He made sure to use his tongue, and I knew he did this on purpose.

"Damn, I hate seeing you like this."

We took our seats, and he sat on the side of me.

"I'm okay, babe."

"No, you ain't. Shit, it looks like all these bitches sick. I just saw the homie leaving going back to the unit. His wife sick as fuck."

"Yeah, I don't know what's going around, but this shit deadly. My mom called me, and when I told her how I was feeling, I cried. This cold got me defeated."

"How she doing?"

"She's good."

"You told her you 'bout to marry me?"

"No."

"So when you gon' tell her? I mean, when she hears my name, she gon' know exactly who I am. My government name and my street name all through that paperwork."

"I don't know. I'mma tell her one day," I replied, and he grabbed my hand.

Chaotic and I sat and talked. Because I was so sick, I couldn't move around like normally, so he got up to get his food. I didn't have an appetite, so I just drank a Monster hoping it gave me a little energy. I wasn't up for playing any games or going outside, so we sat at the table. He kept kissing me, purposely breaking the prison rules. By the time the visit was over, all I wanted to do was crawl in my bed. Chaotic and I kissed goodbye and departed. He watched me all the way out the gate and down the small flight of stairs.

On the way to my car, I noticed the same female officer leaning on a vehicle next to mine. She had a weird look on her face that I tried to ignore. I opened my door and watched her out the side of my eye as she came to the driver side. She wasn't wearing her uniform. Instead, she wore black slacks and a cargo sweater.

"So how's Chaotic?" she asked with a smirk.

"Shit, you work here. You tell me." I stopped to mug her.

"Did you guys get table forty-two today?"

"Bitch, that ain't yo' business." I walked closer to her agitated.

At this point, I didn't give a fuck about her being a cop. I swear I would lay this hoe out right here on the prison's property.

"No need to get nasty with me. Get nasty with your nigga. He's the one going around sticking his dick in everything. Oh, and just so you know, table forty-two ain't the only place where the finger bangs go on downstairs." She chuckled and walked away.

She climbed into her car, and I stood here furious. She quickly backed out and waved sarcastically as she passed by me. I got into my car and sat here. I was tryna process what she had just said wondering if it was true. I thought about the visit the day she was watching Canyon and me. I had a gut feeling something wasn't right, but I didn't sweat it. Chaotic and I were doing things we weren't supposed to, but now that I thought about it, why didn't she say anything that day? I also thought of when I told him how she had looked at me his demeanor changed.

I pulled my phone from under the seat and sent him a text to call me. Instead, he began texting me saying the officers were walking around, so he couldn't be on the phone.

After a few texts, he began calling.

"Man, that bitch lying, ma," he defended soon as I answered.

"Nigga, that bitch ain't lying. That's why she was looking at me like that on the last visit."

"I swear I haven't fucked that hoe."

"She didn't say y'all fucked. She basically said you finger banged her."

"I ain't do—"

"Get on the ground, now!" I heard the voice of a man, and it wasn't Chaotic.

"Get the phone. Search the cell!" Again I heard the male's voice, and I knew then it was officers.

The phone had begun moving around, but I didn't hang up. I wanted to listen for any signs of them physically abusing him. My heart was literally sitting in my stomach.

"Can I just tell my wife what's going on?" I heard Chaotic say, and one of the officers replied no.

Shortly after, the phone went dead, and I became a nervous wreck. Damn.

Chapter 22 Chaotic

Ten Minutes Prior

A nigga was feeling good. I had just gotten back from my visit, and I made a quick two bands that I was gon' give my mother to put up with the rest of the money for Amor's ring. Although I had asked her to marry me, I wanted to lace her finger with a rock. The day I got out was the day I wanted to marry her, then we would have a huge wedding following.

I noticed she had been wearing the ring from her last nigga, and although it wasn't a marriage ring, I wanted it gone. I had already found a ring, and this was the last change I needed to add to it. I pulled my phone out and sent my mom a text to tell her check her green dot. I also informed her to go get the ring first thing to-morrow. Suddenly, a text came through from Amor.

I shook my head knowing exactly who she was referring to; Ms. Rodriguez. I swear that bitch wanted to play, so I had something in store for her. As soon as I caught her this time, I was gon' beat her ass. I dialed Amor's number, and the moment I heard the background noise, I didn't give her a chance to talk.

"Man, that bitch lying, ma."

"Nigga, that bitch ain't lying. That's why she was looking at me like that on the last visit."

"I swear I haven't fucked that hoe." I tried hard to make her understand that bitch was lying.

"She didn't say y'all fucked. She basically said you finger banged her!"

"I ain't do—" I went to say but stopped in my tracks because the guards were running down on me.

I didn't have time to do shit. They already had their guns drawn and were coming through the gate.

"Get on the ground, now! Get the phone. Search the cell!" an officer yelled out and another tackled me to the ground.

"Can I just tell my wife what's going on?" I asked, hoping he'd let me just tell Amor what was going on.

Of course he denied my ass and grabbed the phone. He disconnected the line, which told me she was still holding on listening. They began tearing my cell up, and another officer cuffed me and walked me out. I wasn't worried about them finding shit because I didn't keep my work in my cell. However, getting caught with this phone would get my visits terminated, and my phone privileges restricted for ninety days.

"Aye, Gomez, where's Ms. Rodriguez?" I asked an officer who was always cooler than the others.

He was one of those officers who just did his job and didn't bother us. As long as we weren't doing bullshit, he would sit in his office and mind his business.

"She was transferred. You watch that girl." He nodded his head once, and the look in his eyes told me she was the one who had dropped a dime on me. *Damn.*

Sixty Days Later

There is a new deadly virus surfacing all over the world called Coronavirus. President Trump and other federal leaders initially claimed that the virus would not be a major problem, but many changed their stance, and the virus was declared a national emergency. One by one, states are issuing a stay-at-home order to shut down all non-essential businesses, travel, and gatherings creating a ripple effect that cripples the American economy for months to come. Still, relatively little is understood about the disease, and politicians on both sides of the aisle, as well as leading public health officials, issued guidance, including about mask-wearing that is out of step with what we now know. So far, we have 4,748 new cases in the US leaving 357 dead. Symptoms may appear two-fourteen days after exposure to the virus. People with these symptoms may have

COVID-19:

Fever or chills
Cough
Shortness of breath or difficulty breathing
Fatigue
Muscle or body aches
Headache
New loss of taste or smell
Sore throat
Congestion or runny nose
Nausea or vomiting

Diarrhea

For the last two months, a nigga had been stuck in the cell; no phone, no recreation, and watching the news. Some shit called Covid-19 had surfaced that required them to shut down all prisons. We were on a twenty-four-hour lockdown with no mail coming through, and all I could think about was Amor. This sickness made me wonder if that was what Amor had that she brought up here to me.

Soon as she left visiting and my cell got raided, I was so sick that all I ordered from the commissary was meds. I had a bad ass cough for three weeks after, and if that was how Amor felt, my heart went out to baby girl because that shit wasn't no joke. I finally had gotten over my cough, but my breathing was still tricky. There were rumors surfacing around the prison that inmates with less than a year or nonviolent crimes could be released, but like I said, that was a rumor.

Not being able to talk to Amor had me stressed out. I knew she was still mad at me because our last conversation didn't get resolved. All I wanted her to do was understand that bitch was lying. True, I got my dick sucked, but that was because I was in my feelings. Once Amor was officially mine, all that had changed. I would never do anything to lose her.

What frustrated me more was, I couldn't get ahold of Ms. Rodriguez. She had transferred to another prison. During my integration, Gomez informed me she had told them I had a cell phone and drugs in my cell. That bitch was tryna get me washed up, but she failed. I wasn't no dummy. I knew better than to keep work in my cell. Now as far as the phone, fucking with Amor was how I got caught slipping. I knew it wasn't the right time, so I kept it stashed. The only reason I pulled it out was to tell my mother I sent the money and to get the ring. Then when I saw Amor's text, that was what made me keep it out.

Just like I knew, they suspended my visits and took my phone calls. Really didn't matter because this pandemic had hit and everyone was on the same restrictions as me. While Ms. Ro-driguez thought she was doing something, I already had my nig-gas waiting on her on a nother yard. Her karma was coming when she least expected it, and when word got back to me she was dead, then I would be satisfied.

Chapter 23 Amor

I thought that from this heartache
I could escape
But I fronted long enough to know
There ain't no way
And today
I'm officially missing you

I lay in my bed with tears pouring onto my pillow. I stared at the ring on my ring finger that Chaotic had bought me, and oh, how I wish I could've just told him thank you and I loved him. Since the day they raided his cell, I hadn't heard from him.

The next week, I called to try and schedule a visit, but they told me his visits were restricted, along with his phone privileges for ninety days.

It had been four months of misery, and still no word from him. I knew he was probably thinking I was still mad at him, but I couldn't be because I missed his ass too much. However, he still had some explaining to do, and I was just gon' punch his ass in the gut if I found out what the cop bitch said was true.

Knowing he was in that prison with her had my stomach turning. What if it was true? What if he had her in the broom closet somewhere bent over? I knew I watched too many movies, but nah, that shit went down in prisons, and them CO bitches were thirsty. Chaotic was fine as fuck with power, so I knew they lusted over him. I swear I would shoot him and that bitch.

I quickly shook the thoughts off my mind because the way this new Covid disease was set up, I was sure the guards weren't allowed around the inmates. It was spreading and fast. I had been keeping up with the news, and inside the prisons were affected with the virus worse than the streets. Often, I wondered if the cold I had was related to the virus because I had those same symptoms. If it was, I thanked God because people were dying from it, and I was a survivor.

Right now, the world was on a twenty-four-hour stay home order, and because I had to protect Heaven, I wouldn't go any-where. Ru was on his way with tissue and water for us, so I wouldn't have to leave. I used Instacart to deliver groceries, and we ordered food from DoorDash most days. Because it was only Heaven and I, it was easy to maintain, but being locked away was starting to drive me crazy. Ru popped in and out, but for the most part, he was always in the hood. Before he pulled up, I was gonna hurry and write Chaotic a letter in hopes it made it to him.

To: My Husband (Big Poppa)
From: Your Wife (Gutta Baby)

Dear Chaotic,

This is gonna be the last letter I send because you haven't responded to the other 8 letters I've sent. I don't know if you call yourself being mad, have you been in trouble or is it this pandemic that's stopping you from communicating with me. Whatever it is, I pray you're okay. I love you and miss you so much. Yes I'm mad at you but that's something we will deal with later. Right now I just need to know if you're okay? I got the ring from your mother and oh my God it's beautiful. It only added anticipation to us getting married. I'm waiting for the day to become your wife and I'll wear your last name proudly. Canyon, I pray to God you haven't deceived me with that bitch in there. That shit will kill me. I really don't wanna talk about it, I just hope to see you soon so I can punch you in the gut and we can get over it. I love you. Don't ever forget that, okay?

P.S. All I'm doing is, Loving you & Missing you!

Always yours, Amor.

Once I was done writing, I put the letter into an envelope and sealed it. I ran outside and dropped it into the outgoing mail, and I made it just in time because Ru was pulling in. I helped him into the house with the bags, and I noticed he had brought Wingstop. I set the bags down and washed my hands, then went to get Heaven from her playpen.

Ru began to make our plates, so I put the baby in her high chair, then took a seat at the table. I handed Heaven her chicken and fries and watched how excited she was for the chicken. I grabbed a piece of lemon pepper chicken and dipped it into the mild sauce, then took a bite.

"Nice ring," Ru said from across the table.

I looked down to my ring but ignored him.

"You got married?"

"No, I ain't got married, Ruger. It's a promise ring. Something like the one you had bought me," I replied sarcastically. "Ru, why you always so worried about me and what I got going on with my nigga? You got a bitch."

"I ain't got shit."

"Nigga, you think the streets don't talk? Trust me, I've gotten screen shots with you posting yo' new bitch. Guess what I tell everyone? That's his business. I don't be all in yo' mix, so stay out mine. What we had is over, so accept mine like I gotta accept yours."

"I ain't gotta accept shit."

"Well, stop coming around."

I left it at that and took another bite from my food. Ru had me fucked up. He had a new bitch he was posting on the 'Gram, and a couple people had sent me the screen shots. I always told them it was Ru's business because I really didn't care. I had moved on and was happy. I always hoped he found the same happiness. Shit, I couldn't make him happy, so hopefully, she did a better job because Chaotic was damn sure doing a wonderful job at securing his spot.

Just the attention alone was more than I've ever gotten from Ru. The boutique and just the overall love. Ru barely told me he loved me. I heard the shit from Chaotic daily. This man made me happy, and the trip part it was, from a fucking prison bunk.

Ding!

The doorbell rang pulling Ru and I's attention.

"It's prolly UPS," I assumed because since this pandemic, all I had to do was online shop.

"I got it." Ru stood to his feet. He wandered off toward the living room and to the front door. He stayed gone for a few minutes, so I figured they needed my signature or ID.

I got up from the table and wiped my hands. I headed for the door, and Ru's tall frame was blocking it. Suddenly, I noticed his gun in his hand but hanging down to his side. It made me walk further into the living room, and when I was near the door, my heart stopped. I clutched my mouth as my head tilted to the side. It was like time had frozen, and the adrenaline racing through my body had my heart pumping.

Chaotic stood there with a cold mean-mug, and just like Ru, he had his gun in his hand hanging down to his side. His eyes dismissed Ruger's and wandered down my body. I was wearing only a t-shirt and a pair of socks. He instantly frowned, but fuck this shirt. What the fuck was he doing home?

"'Sup, Cute Face?"

TO BE CONTINUED!

Barbie Amor Book Trap
https://www.facebook.com/groups/1624522544463985/

Visit My Website
http://authorbarbiescott.com/?v=7516fd43adaa

Like My Page On Facebook
https://www.facebook.com/
AuthorBarbieScott/?modal=composer

Instagram:
https://www.instagram.com/Authorbarbieamor/

CPSIA information can be obtained
at www.ICGtesting.com
Printed in the USA
LVHW021927240222
711933LV00010B/1185